D1546843

THE SKIN TEAM

The Skin Team
© 2016 Jordaan Mason

Published by Magic Helicopter Press
Portland, OR & Pioneer Valley, MA
www.magichelicopterpress.com

Reproduction of selections from this book, for non-commercial personal or educational purposes, is permitted and encouraged, provided the Author and Publisher are acknowledged in the reproduction. Reproduction for sale, rent, or other use involving financial transaction is prohibited except by permission of the Author and Publisher.

This novel is a work of fiction. Names, characters, places, and incidents are the products of the author's imagination or are used fictitiously, and any resemblance to actual persons, living or dead, events or locales is entirely coincidental.

Thank you to the editors of the following journals, where portions of *The Skin Team* originally appeared: *Red Lightbulbs, The Scrambler, NOÖ Journal, Unsaid.*

ISBN: 978-0-9841406-4-0
Cataloging-in-Publication Data available from the Library of Congress

2 4 6 8 9 7 5 3 1 0
First edition, June 2013
Second edition, December 2015

Cover art and design by Tarsila Stoeckicht
Book design by Mike Young
Set in Fanwood Text (by Barry Schwartz) and Vevey (by Vanessa Lam)

THE SKIN TEAM

A NOVEL BY
JORDAAN MASON

MAGIC HELICOPTER PRESS
PORTLAND, OR & PIONEER VALLEY, MA

The child has no sexuality in the eyes of parents.

Tony Duvert

THE POWER IS OUT, SING

The thing that you must understand is that children will do terrible things if you leave them alone long enough. Sarah kissed me for the first time just after a swimming lesson. We exchanged chlorine. She said that the pool was our orphanage now. She said all I was to her was salt, something to keep her occupied while chewing, and at the time I figured she meant it. I said I preferred pepper, sneezing, letting the dogs bite me. I let one hang off my face for almost three minutes once. A dog I mean. They put it to sleep even though I told them that I had asked for it. After all that time running through the corn fields and sleeping in the barn, waiting for it to happen. Her mouth left red sores on mine. She took all the water from my body and gave it back to the lake. I told everyone it was a cold sore. I told them all the scars I had on me were from dogs.

We both had houses that slept, separately. The Power Company Building was very close, caught beside a road, parallel to a pond where I fed ducks too much bread. Sarah told me that if I listened hard enough I would hear the energy. All of the grass was charged with it, like everything around me was language waiting to happen. She said it was all just the Power Company Building. We were so close to what we wanted to be. I told her I wanted to be a poet but I was tired of words. She told me to listen to the power cables and not talk anymore.

He said he would meet me there that night, and we could find cheaper ways to get drunk. I told him I was not thirsty, he said: I know, that's not what I mean. He cut three lines into the side of my stomach with a pocketknife and kissed my neck for a long time while we waited for the energy to fill us. Our arms gave out. He didn't take his rollerblades off, only his t-shirt.

I never got his stains out no matter how much bleach I drank. She didn't notice how much I smelled like him. Her stomach was my stomach: what flames I swallowed, she did too.

I stood in her bedroom with a glass of milk and tried to memorize the route I'd taken to get there. From her house to my house. From the treehouse in the woods to his front door. I wanted to stop drawing maps, but they insisted on paper. They documented everything but kept it hidden, scattered. So that maybe someone could track us, but they would never know how to fit it all together. Even the three of us forgot, speaking our own languages in the corners of rooms, with some of the fingers of our hands just barely intact on us, spoiled in our mouths.

It was easy for all these silent treatments, for the secrets to conjure residue up to our neckline, straighten the church pews, gift wrap the slaughter. When we wanted to sing, there were songs, and when we wanted to be quiet, there was the energy.

I told Sarah that I didn't want to see an actual map of where we lived because I liked that I never knew where north was. I said: *the map is not the territory*, which I had read in a book. She said she was going to get it tattooed on her stomach, every road, so every time I would have to see it. For this and for other reasons, I mostly kept the lights off.

She told me that if when you are angry you happen upon it, you should always tear away what you can, even if just ditch water, even if just a company pen. This is how she justified her lack of chronology. We crawled in through the window the same night that her mother finally found sleep—in the bathroom, with the light still on, the water still running. Her mouth was never darker, open.

Sarah said it was what she always wanted, and the only sad thing was that she had to do it herself.

We would sit by the highway fence and wait for the energy to find us first. It was a game we played, almost like *hide-and-seek*, except that we were never It. I counted the amount of metal in her mouth and in the cars. We couldn't keep track of our speed, so we sold our identification cards for more ginger, for more noise. The metal in her mouth lessened over time. She asked me to pull my penis out, and said: What do you want me to do to it.

I said it was up to her. I said: You make the decisions from now on, okay.

She pulled her hair tight into a braid and then around my neck, like so. My stomach heavy with brickwork. I remember the emergency room, then: swollen so suddenly in me. And she put her hands between my legs and held onto me hard, her eyes changing colour. And what is a girl without a mother doing touching me between my legs, I wonder. What does our death even mean.

She left the attic in the night and left me to sleep afterwards. That's what this dream is: always waiting in the dark to be alone again.

In the closet we lit cigarettes and had a skin riot. We blued each other green and left rings around each other's eye sockets, mine in his. Our Bible studies were us raking the weather from the yard, putting our hands inside of one another—the only place that it was warm some nights. The way his body bent back was a true testament to how badly he wanted. I would mount him and hold his hipbones, and he would recite the Lord's Prayer, all of his holes open, trying to receive god.

After the hush there was hardly any resolution. All we needed was the hum to keep going, something dull to depend on. The mattress in the crawlspace was rubbed clean with butter, desk drawers against the walls filled with seeds that could never be gardened. The same way we shared fluid—all of it kept in pockets, unfertilized.

Underneath the parkbench, Sarah passed me an Oreo cookie and a poem she had written about us. One line in it compared us to being in a laundry machine for eternity, and I thought: goddamn you, what pelt is enough. We are too close to a graveyard for you to give me a machine like this. We are too close to our quiet to believe in songs.

Waiting for the bus, there was a sign that said *Free Parking*, and I thought: well, if it's free.

I first felt the sickness in my stomach after losing most of my weekly allowance at the racetrack. I did my best to explain this to a doctor but she needed more information about what kind of a pain it was. I described it to her as: my stomach is going blind, I can't taste anything except ash, do you think that I swallowed fire while I was sleeping, is that possible. She gave me a stern look and asked if it was a stabbing pain or a throbbing pain. I said it was dull right like my stomach was going blind, I can't see the food I am digesting or taste it, just ash. She did a complete physical and said that everything was fine and I just needed to be sleeping better. I said how am I supposed to do that if I am swallowing fire in my sleep. She prescribed sleeping pills to be taken *as needed*, even if I was swallowing fire in the night. I counted on the fact that Sarah was swallowing it, too—all of us, together.

We sat cross-legged in the hospital waiting room staring at a woman with braids in her hair. She was holding a green towel around her arm, crying with every crack in her face, every small crevice that we longed to sleep in. When she was finally called in, I did not know how to accept the silence of the room, the tired faces of mothers.

I told him that if I were to film this moment, I would prefer that the soda machine be Coke rather than Pepsi, not because of any preference in taste, but because red looks more intense on screen. He did not say anything. He did not hold my hand. They called my name first.

Have you ever been tested for the HIV virus before, the woman asked, fixing her blouse.

No, I said, and I don't like needles okay.

The first time she took off all of her clothes for me was in her childhood room. Her father was just through the wall, snoring loud, a row of dolls nestled on a shelf all glaring at me, the swelled purple of the room dampening my mouth. She wanted to ash herself away; I wanted to turn the lamp off. I never asked her to undress; she did it because she wanted to, because she needed a reason to fall asleep later, to heave, to pass, to be filled up with sound and semen.

I did not fill her with either that night, only air.

Him and I were ignorant of how to enter one another, so for a long time we were just naked, moving bodies, and eventually, come. When we finally achieved it he was seven hundred pounds of salt, I was many favourite bones. I wanted to erase table manners from our heads, to forget that we were two people. He swallowed what little I gave him. Before that all we did was tug. All that blood in us swarming so much we were weightless. It was an organic skill, lacked prowess but professed instantly.

Her mother made apple pancakes and re-arranged the dining room so that there was enough room for me to sit at the table with her family. Her father sipped at coffee, fixed his tie, ate sliced white bread with butter. It was not toasted. We did not talk but I shared the same harbour as him—I suddenly knew what it meant to be illegible. Her mother spent most of the night returning to the kitchen to scrub the batter off the frying pan, repeatedly.

She jumped into the lake and I followed her. We rode our bicycles all afternoon and ate red rope licorice in the field behind the pine woods. Our clothes were wet since we had left them on. We were painted with dried brown grass and magnolia petals. She said she could not feel the energy when we were in the field; we were too far away from it. I kissed her on the cheek and said: But I am right here.

She accused me of not having enough electricity. She even avoided having me touch her, and if I tried to, she would fight me off. This is the only time she was openly angry with me, only a hint of violence, and this is when I finally wanted her. I took her, then, the way I took him.

I passed out in the field singing a song about New Jersey. I told him I wanted to be Peter Pan. I told him I wanted us to keep fucking forever, that I wanted to be his mother, to cut his hair and call him in for supper. He was the first to throw up. His arms did it, too.

She passed the cigarette back to me and said: Well, what are your desert island records.Like that was such a casual question, like she really wanted to know.

I said: Sarah, I don't listen to music, just energy, and you know that.

I saw her following the train tracks in the opposite direction of the river, leaving pages from her journal behind her as she moved. I didn't bother trying to follow her. I let the birds do that. She halted under the bridge for three and a half minutes, staring at the bare book in her hands, and then disappeared around the corner.

I found eight pages of her journal on the tracks and three in the gutter next to the bowling alley. The rest had scattered elsewhere. I found only one line that mentioned her mother's death. She wrote: *we found her together.*

There I was, too, collecting them all up, keeping her fragments in my pockets while I walked around the buildings, all of them collapsing slowly. There was still the sore taste of milk in my mouth, stuck to my gums, the faint taste of dandelions from my fingers, from pulling them out of the ground as I crowned the edge of the train yard. I heard music far away, coming from the woods.

In one of the abandoned trains, he and I made a pact with one another. We spit into our hands and rubbed them together, like a handshake. It tasted like dandelions. He said: This spit is sacred spit, this handshake holy. We continued to trade it, the music still somewhere, the pages of her journal poking out of my pockets, all while he took off my pants as quickly as he could.

The treehouse was filled with lamps powered by long orange extension cords stretching from one of the exterior plugs of my house, around the shed and into the woods. There were nine of them attached together to achieve this length, and therefore we could have fifteen lamps plugged in simultaneously. From far away, the treehouse looked like the hub of a thousand fireflies. Maybe a fire but no smoke, only wood and floral curtains. The treehouse itself was constructed from discarded pieces of whatever we could find, wandering the woods where the brush had grown in too much, our legs covered in scars. We found splinters of old wood as if houses had just fallen from the sky, littering the earth. We filled wagons and wheelbarrows. We had this obsession: creating a space outside of our homes, temporary houses scattered around the town. All of them were at some point in time destroyed—either by us intentionally, or other local kids looking for anything to do in the middle of the night, or by natural causes: seasons changing, rust, water, fire, being too sick to stand, sing, or sleep. These spaces, however impermanent, kept us going, running on the engine oil of the lightning stark purple in the polluted sky, explosions of thunder right above us, all the while the lake being brought right back down on our heads, us raving through the woods at night like we didn't have anywhere else to go.

I had no idea what was causing the sickness. The doctors couldn't seem to detect it and therefore they were no good to me. All I knew was that the Power Company Building was involved. I knew this primarily because of what I remembered as *chronology*. As in: *this* happened and then *this* happened. From what I could remember, or at least from what my stomach could remember, the sickness only started after I felt the energy. He told me once that it was all because of North. He said: Look it up. I did my best to research the subject without looking at any maps (this being done by covering the image portion of the texts with my hands so that all I could obtain and hold in my head were the words) and came to this conclusion: the sickness was a direct result of the magnetic energy of the earth pulling my body towards North. As if it could actually be plotted out and I could be pulled towards poles. As in: my stomach was full of undigested metal, it was going blind, I wanted to go North. I gathered all of this with what I remembered as *logic*. What I couldn't understand for a long time was what any of that had to do with the energy. I spent a lot of time at the Power Company Building, sneaking out of the window of my bedroom at night and wandering the grounds. What should be noted here is the level of *exploration* that would happen during these times, i.e. how my body found many ways to experience the energy depending on where I was in relation to the building. One night I figured out how to make the stomach ache go away, even if just momentarily.

If I laid flat on it—my stomach—directly between the two main generators at the Power Company Building, then I could not feel the sickness. All of the metal in my stomach was charged with electricity, at the exact right voltage, and it no longer hurt at all. I thought about what would have happened if, somehow, I could fit lightbulbs in my mouth properly, if I could charge them enough to light up. There weren't spare lightbulbs in the house for me to ever test out this possibility without my mother noticing they were gone, knowing her pantry habits, but I was certain that if I could get my hands on them, I could charge them. If I moved from that position at all—onto my back, for example—my stomach went blind again, and I could feel North everywhere. In the graveyard across the street, waist-deep in water, pulling burnt patches of skin from my body, I could feel the sickness full on. So I spent a lot of time there at night, just like that, to dull the pain for a little while. This was a temporary solution. I kept this a secret from both him and her, as in I did not speak about it very frequently with what I remembered as *language*. I told him that mostly I could only taste what I had devoured long after it had left my body, like aftershock. I said: I am swallowing fire while I am asleep. I wanted his violence because I thought if I caused enough violence to the body then the sickness would have to leave me. Then there was the fire: all of the energy stopped and the stomach ache went away entirely.

SYNESTHESIA

NOW THEN

Three blind mice got the knives out in the barn. North is just a territory, briefly between breaths. If you do not consider how much eating is being had, most of this is true. If you do not consider that gasoline is free if you put it in your mouth first, or that there is feral energy being passed around, having conversations about trout, taking bananas from your kitchen, then dawn is quiet. All sound has escaped and there is nothing there except for the light hum of the energy, which is enough to make you blind, if you listen long enough. Three did so, that is went blind, and yes all three broken from a single seed, all sleeping in separate beds but only all simultaneously for about forty-six minutes. A seed scatters between what is left of beds and bedding, replanted in parts of the churchyard, the basketball courts, as swimmers and hunters, as you. All three are fragments of one larger whole, barely distinguishable from one another. One: a boy with pursed ears (possibly from being burnt or drowned, as in there is this ringing but what from) and swallowed metal holding his gut basically (like a hug, only tighter and more constant). In this instance (and only in this instance) we will call him Synesthesia. Two: a girl who has lakes inside her as blood, who snapped the birds from the white water fresh and went off singing proud about it long afterwards. We'll call her Sarah. That's not her real name, but the one you'd carve onto a gravestone if you had to do it. Three: a boy spent all night hunting at the truck stop and making fires in the forest with only his bare hands and the bones of old trees. In this instance (and only in this instance) we will call him Kinesthesia. One is the number of suns in the sky cooking the lake water as it juts over the horizon; two is the number of packages lost in the mail that morning never making it to two front doors; three is the number of separate bodies in one coffin eventually, as all things come back together eventually, as all fluids and all solids are made up of parts eventually, as all cleaned houses are emptied or filled eventually, all skin eventually, wood eventually, a bug bite on your dog's underside eventually, a power out. At some point in time, it will happen. As all good and sinister as it may sound. If things are meant to converge they will do so when all things speak in perfect union, when all terror comes from the same place and is being made right around you. What you believe to be singular will in fact multiply, fracture. This exact point on the earth, fractured. All three are made up of other parts which are also fragments of the earth speaking with tongues too big for their mouths. Several of these parts have been unionized by the natural order of life into other beings, which are as follows: the Power Company Building, Moving Water, Erosion, Other Alterations, Thermal Energy, The Efficient Use Of Land, Continuous Operation, North, and True North. All of these names being given by that language which exists amongst some talkers. All of these are wanderers who have each had their own interactions with one another and are all related, if not genetically then through struggle, upheaval, and overall conduct in regards to their existence and how they affect what is known as all other living things.

THE "IT" DISEASE

Schools of children are waiting in line for their laundry so they can breathe again. One girl and one boy swap their received clothes and organize them according to size, colour, fabric, fashion statement. The boys are all running into the sweltering woods and splitting into teams for hide and go seek. The girls are not allowed to play. They decide on their teams according to which colour of clothing each boy has the most of: Red, Green, Blue, Yellow, Orange, and Purple. Boys count to three and then run in separate directions, primary colours in one direction, secondary in another. The Oranges are It first. The girls do not have a game that they play, but they sit in the park singing songs to one another. Wrestling as old tigers.

THE POWER COMPANY BUILDING

The energy (read: that which is the violent and comforting sound of the Power Company Building, the long lovesong carved on the bottoms of boats, sifting through the houses in all of the walls, into lamps, televisions, microwaves, stereo systems, refrigerators, et al.) is one soft solid made for human bellies, all that which is transmitted from heaven into the holes we leave open for filling. The Power Company Building is the dear friend you forgot you had, the one you need gnawing on you. Momentary brownouts are nothing to worry about. They are just a simple sneeze. Sit tight. There is going to be fire.

BEFORE

The day starts like this: the farmyards are tilted and spread across the fields, almost stale. All the bread for the mouths of birds and boys being baked in large ovens by men and women who listen to the heat. All of the choirs are singing thick and sweet, polished across the rooftops of all the houses. The Efficient Use Of Land, fat-bellied, stuck out, untucked, is moaning off-key the hymn of the choir—the drunk in the back of the ballroom, a garish tart full of wine. And the song goes: We are all accidents. The Power Company Building is holding Synesthesia by the wrists, slapping his face to wake him up, to make him sing, but he is quiet, still. He tumbles from bed to tub, rinses out the charcoal from his mouth, drowning out the swallowed sun from his sleep. His wrists are in the living room, which is flooding, again and again. The choirs are in the train stations, the post offices, the stomachs of the police. Anything to warn the authorities: it is happening. Another accident, us. Another foul mouth filled with fire. And the bathtub is trying to drown him so he won't have to see it. Moving Water is restless because it knows what is coming. The horses, too—dry, looking for ways to get to the lake. Sarah wakes up next: a routine of pretending to brush the hair but instead just pulling it out on purpose. Other Alterations gathers all of the perfect colours of fabric for the day to fit her body. She is unaware of how sick the horses are, how sick he is, or that it is being transferred between all of them, slowly. This is the kind of thing she can't feel no matter how harsh the energy is or how much she keeps quiet. Her breakfast is hard-scraped jam on toast and a vanilla yogurt cup. His large intestine is wrapped tightly around her head like too much of a scarf. Kinesthesia wakes up last—he can hear the choirs more distinct than the others. His head is pealing with them. All that sleeping did him no good. The Efficient Use Of Land outweighs them all. His interference almost makes it impossible for the choirs to be heard correctly, but they are vehement: accidents are necessary sometimes.

MOVING WATER

Moving Water has been gambling on the horses. Not for money but for blood. Moving Water says: I will eat all of the horses. And: I want no one to win. Sarah is surrounded by horses running in the surf. Her mother is standing thigh-deep in the water with her mouth open. The horses are circling her mother and kicking up their legs high near her. Sarah does not have a physical body and therefore cannot chase them down. She is a voyeur only in this moment. Erosion and Moving Water, both of whom to her are unfamiliar, are in between the horses and her mother, trying to separate them. Moving Water is trying to drown the horses. Erosion is just the sand dulling down until the horses start sinking. And one by one, they all go under, disappearing completely, her mother watching. Sarah's mother doesn't flinch, staying still as each horse is sunk into the sand.

BEFORE

Synesthesia goes into his father's room and checks through the dresser drawers for some money to use later in the day on horses. The telephone sings instead of his head for once. It is Sarah, wondering if they are going to walk to the park later. She has a poem she wants to read to him. Moving Water already has the poem memorized, pulling through its wave hair, reciting the lines again and again in tides, in terror. The Efficient Use Of Land is rubbing itself against Moving Water near the throat region accusing it of illegitimate children, and it turns to the Power Company Building and says: How much of you is solid and how much of you is going to come apart? To which it replies with volts cracking into slices of fruit: I am all solid from my head to my toes and also walking weatherward, staying in place, protecting my family from fires or trying to. The Efficient Use Of Land and Moving Water can see the embarrassment, the harsh redness, in the Power Company Building's face. Synesthesia drinks ten glasses of water before leaving the house. This is common morning practice for him: a way to dull the stomach ache for a while, to clean out all that sat inside him through the night. His wrists, which are not technically his wrists, are rug-burned red, and he is sore, smiling. Sarah and Synesthesia meet at the park with a box of Oreo cookies and her poem, which she recites to him, twice, the worms in the ground trying to listen, Erosion trying to purge the worms, Other Alternations trying to plagiarize the poem and sell it to high school English teachers everywhere. It is hard to plagiarize a poem that is being read aloud, though, because where are the line-breaks? The animals gather at the edge of the forest and watch the boys sneak around the pines and maples, trying to find good hiding spots. Moving Water wants to snatch them whole from the ground. Sarah asks Synesthesia if he likes the poem, to which he replies: It is wonderful; is it about me? And she says: Yes, of course, it is about you, you & I forever & ever the way that it should be and no one else. Kinesthesia has followed both of them and is around the brush where the boys are hiding and the animals are gathering. He is close enough to catch only the most casual pieces of the conversation. He also tries to memorize the poem, but only because he wishes to use it against her at a later date, one he has not yet picked. The choirs in his head have started a hand-clap rhythm that goes: stomp foot constant every quarter note, pause hands, clap three eighth notes (all in ¾ time), but the words have not changed: *We are all accidents dee-dee-dee.* A trumpet, which is part of the choir, which is the human voice made from the brass of the mouth and hands that were had, plays interludes when they are getting tired in the legs and forearms, bruises forming, a break for water, for air, to clean the lungs out. True North—which is above all of them, who created the choir in the first place, who has always had his hands around the neck of the Power Company Building holding it red and royally, who once fucked and left the Efficient Use Of Land for Moving Water and created consistent quarrel between them for this reason, who banished Erosion to be in the ground, who caused Other Alterations into being without giving it a proper place or even purpose (mostly just can you cut the grass and who will feed the horses), who told the tectonic plates when and where to shift, who waits impatiently in Synesthesia's sick stomach, and who overall has the compass and is biting it down hard between charred bone of the mouth region—already knows the poem by heart because True North wrote the poem a long time ago, under sinks of lava and under the attempted sacrifice of North, who is his false adopted brother, a teether with his head glued to the ground. A poem, however, is not enough to kill a direction, even if that direction is false, and even if that direction lives under the pretense of being the Official and True direction to follow and to use as a guiding point but obviously isn't at all True and doesn't even warrant having the word True in his proper name.

EROSION

This part of the earth is cracked and moving, moving nowhere, where is it going, see the thing is I am already losing my way. And who am I? Who am I to be lost among fractures of earth?

BEFORE

Synesthesia wanders away from the park into the woods to
the spot where he is supposed to meet Kinesthesia at eleven o'clock
(for which he is nineteen minutes late, which is not a problem
considering Kinesthesia is, on average, thirty-three minutes late,
and exactly that on this particular day). The rendezvous point
is a row of three trees which have all grown into one another,
their branches overlapping intermittently. Scattered around
them are piles of old mattresses, burned yellow from piss and
other fluids, bleached from sun, dulled from rain. This is the spot
where they first had one another. Synesthesia arrives and waits
out the remaining fourteen minutes for Kinesthesia, smoking
two cigarettes in the interval (one immediately as soon as he sits
down, and one four minutes after finishing the first). They do not
embrace or say hello. Kinesthesia sits down next to one of the
three trees. Neither of them speak for another twelve minutes,
although both of them smoke one cigarette separately each, and
then they split one, which Kinesthesia initiates, pulls out, offers,
and lights. What horse won the last race last night, Kinesthesia
finally says to break the silence. Moving Water says: All of the
horses lost; I am swallowing them as we speak, which neither of
them seems to hear. I don't remember its name—something about
Ruckus, Synesthesia replies, then: I didn't bet though, I didn't
have any money, my dad's wallet was empty. Kinesthesia says to

him: I heard we're all accidents. They look at one another for a long time after he says this, neither of them speaking again for another four and a half minutes, at which point in time they both start to remove their clothing. True North watches all of this happening at once because True North is omnipotent, and despite the fact that it is a direction in itself, it can see things happening from all directions at once, from any point on the earth. It is the North you know, as in the false brother, who is limited by his direction. The boys fuck and then he pulls out of him. Synesthesia, that is, removes himself from Kinesthesia, leaving liquid inside. The head organ blown out of tissue and swollen silver. Naked is maybe not the right word for the context of their skin at this moment, even though neither of them is wearing clothes. Their clothes are hanging from the branches of trees waiting to be dried, to be back on the bones. Kinesthesia and Synesthesia switch the t-shirts that they were previously wearing since they were in possession of one another's shirts and the borrowing time had run out. They jocularly discuss the matter as if the only reason they came and got naked in the first place was because they needed their clothes back. And Kinesthesia, turning serious, says: Why are they yours or mine anyway—this thread that thread the collar of one to the neckbone of another, they should belong to us all equally. Synesthesia replies: My mother bought me this shirt is why; it's My Mother's Shirt. His Mother's Shirt says: I have always truly been Your Mother's Shirt. Long gap of silence between them, which is instead the noise of a thousand birds trying to eat the leftover meat of seaweed on the shore. True North tucks them all into proverbial beds of old hair from drains, diesel from engines. North tries to hold True North close to him and say: You are my brother and I will always love you. But True North runs his fingernails hard on the head of him and leaves him open to see what comes out. The boys roll over in the dust, drifting.

OTHER ALTERATIONS

Other Alterations is making new dresses out of the old dresses that Sarah tried to leave in a dumpster and on the side of the train tracks, scattered about pinks and blues.

Other Alterations is sitting on the ceiling of her bedroom, holding its own hands and chanting, staring down at the mess of clothes on the floor.

Other Alterations arranges all of the clothes in her bedroom by colour, and then again by size, and then again by fabric, fixing all of the seams of the dresses that are coming loose, re-tying all of the threads, giving them new ends.

Other Alterations cuts up all of Sarah's clothes and sews all the pieces into new clothes, a collection of quilt patchwork.

Other Alterations will you feed the horses, will you cut the grass.

THE "IT" DISEASE

While the two boys are fucking on the forest floor, one of the members from the Orange team and one of the members from the Blue team accidentally cross paths with one another and see them (Synesthesia and Kinesthesia) on the ground, pulling and pushing into one another. The boy on the Blue team stands shocked as he sees this, his face gone white, and the boy from the Orange team shouts out: Blue is It, everybody, Blue is It!, before running off again into the woods. The Blue boy stands inert, staring. What finally catches his attention away from the act is that he sees what appears to be a traveling Red in the distance, which only upon closer inspection would get his team again free from the disease of being It, so he runs.

THERMAL ENERGY

Kinesthesia is in a large red room, which is vacant and dark except for one light hanging low from the ceiling over a circular table with three chairs placed around it—one of which he is seated at, the other two occupied by Thermal Energy and Continuous Operation. The table has a thick layer of dust and ash stuck to it. There are empty and half-empty packs of cigarettes and plastic wrappings, a collection of different match boxes, burnt out matches, a deck of cards, and poker chips. The room is cloaked in smoke, blistering hot. Thermal Energy picks up the deck of cards and starts shuffling them in his hands and the cigarette hanging out of the left side of his mouth makes the words slur together: Am I dealing you in or what? *The light above hums what could have been a song or sound if anyone could hear it.* What's the game, Kinesthesia says. Thermal Energy says: Poker, Texas Hold'em—you in? Kinesthesia says: I don't know how to play poker. Oh it's easy, Continuous Operation pipes in, lighting two cigarettes with one match, handing one of them over to Kinesthesia. Continuous Operation coughs out ash and eventual horse hair: We'll teach you. Kinesthesia shifts around in his seat and tries to remember what he's learned from films about poker, to listen to the light, but can't seem to come up with anything, other than the concept of *bluffing*. He holds the smoke in his lungs for as long as he possibly can until his head starts to feel fuzzy, looking down at the cards in his hands to realize he can barely read them, the hard edges of objects lost. He looks around the table, but the faces won't come into focus. Cards on the table, hands announced. The river has been laid. Thermal Energy has rivers running through him and he runs through rivers, casually, like rivers can be caught running. Kinesthesia tries again to look at his cards, staring at them for a long time, the soft reds and blacks indistinguishable from one another. Thermal Energy play-punches Kinesthesia on the shoulder: Hey come on; it's your turn to show your cards; that's how the game works. He snaps out of it enough to speak: I—I can't see anything. Like: *where is the light when you need it.* Show us the cards and we'll tell you what you've got; just put them on the table, Continuous Operation says. Trembling, Kinesthesia follows their lead, puts his cards down as best he can without seeing, releasing them from his fingers with a snapping sound as they hit the veneer of the table. He waits, blind in smoke, for them to tell him his hand.

NOW THEN?

The energy moves through the forest, hovers over the lake, into the kitchens of the houses of grandmothers and housewives, of husbands without antlers, of children playing chess improperly. It moves through the plumbing systems and comes out of the taps, into the televisions, into the spider dens that sneak in the corners of closets. The Power Company Building, which is still holding Synesthesia by the wrists, is having what it would call a good sharing moment: passing around the hat for anyone to fill it with anything, giving out everything that can be given. That can be created by moving machines, by Moving Water, by Thermal Energy, by Continuous Operation. By smokers' mouths and wind being pulled through tunnels of timbre choir-singing. All of this in earth below you. Underground, you. Following the fault lines to find out where the next transformation of the earth is going to be. Where will the tectonic plates shift to? True North's diary is heavily guarded and sealed and cannot be read, and therefore his decisions, although made far in advance and through very rational consideration, are hard to keep track of, or to know about until it is almost too late. There is so much movement, then, without knowing. So much not knowing. And the three move separately for what might be the last time, the first time.

BEFORE

Synesthesia walks out of the forest, across town, sweating from the sun shining down on him hard, trying to stay underneath the greenery of trees poking out in front yards, passing by the grocery stores, the video rental store, the Chinese restaurant, the burger place, the laundromat. When he gets to the racetrack, he leans on the fence for a while, looking in at them first. There are six horses on harnesses moving around in a circle, getting ready for the next race. He sees Sarah. Mister Lonely moves with the five other harnessed horses. Synesthesia crooks himself over the fence, peels of white paint catching on his pants, showing the old worn wood underneath. He strides across the field from the fence to the stables, passing jockeys on horses and trainers holding the reigns of them, horses grazing but confined by metal posts coming out of the earth, patches of grass that have been beaten into mud, and past the horses circling on harnesses, to where Sarah is standing, filling troughs with feed. He looks past her into the darkness of the individual stalls, most of them empty, the horses all in various places, getting ready for the races, some of them already on the track, some already sleeping back in the lacklight of their rooms. They're not drinking enough water, Sarah says, crossing over to him. He puts his arms on the top of one of the stall doors, looking in, confirming that it is unoccupied, lifting his body and pushing the door forward, swinging it back and forth, occasionally steadying himself by pressing his feet down on the ground again, and pushing off. Maybe there is something wrong with the water, he replies, tension in his voice from the strain of his body swinging. Sarah starts filling a bucket with water from the hose, which is jutting out from the wall on the far side of the stables, watching him swing two stalls up. It's the same water it's always been, she says, sticking her hands in the bucket and moving the water around. Moving Water bellows to no one in particular: I am killing the horses with my bare hands. The Efficient Use Of Land tries to run in circles with the harnessed horses, who are all walking at a regular, relaxed pace. Mister Lonely and the five other horses—Girl Winner, Cloud Nine, Kickin Up Some Ruckus, Garland, and Nijinski—ignore him. They pant what saliva is left in them, Erosion following them under their hoof-prints in the dirt. The Power Company Building has a momentary brownout which is felt only in the east section of town, all of the lights dimming for a moment, and all of the clocks re-setting briefly, except for those which are powered by batteries and/or are worn on the wrist region of the human body. Other Alterations re-sets the clock in her room to the correct time. True North re-sets Kinesthesia's alarm clock to the correct time. All of the other clocks in town are left alone to be fixed by whoever deems it necessary. Sarah and Synesthesia lie down next to one of the horse stables and Sarah puts her hand underneath his shirt, feeling the three equally lengthy scars on him, lightly enough so that she doesn't necessarily draw attention to them. A gunshot goes off in the distance, which means that one of the races has started. Neither of them jumps at the sound. They have both heard it before. Their bodies move away from each other like snails. I'm putting my money on Mister Lonely, Synesthesia says, finally, sitting up from his position and reaching into his pocket, pulling out a couple of dollars. Sarah also sits up, brushing some hay and dirt off of her legs, back, and shoulders, and says: I have to keep feeding the horses but come by again before you leave. He agrees to, leaving the hay in his hair and on his jeans, and starts walking out past the stables, staring up at the large clock on the marquee of the stadium in the distance. Sarah stands and watches him leave, her gut going, before returning to filling buckets with water and moving them around the stables. Other Alterations makes and unmakes her bed, over and over, like a ceremony celebrating nothing.

THE EFFICIENT USE OF LAND

What would a choir sing if a choir could sing and wasn't being held down at all or forced to, wasn't having its mouths held open the entire time. All of the lead in the world solidifies in the bottom of the river bank, yes, it's true, and one farmer tilling the land finds that it's just so easy to move it, and another farmer tilling the land finds that it's just so easy to move it, and seeds grow in threes together beneath the soil, not making a single sound.

BEFORE

Synesthesia puts his ticket in his pocket, nestling in to get as comfortable as possible on the hard wood of the flip-down chair, which is not in any way cushioned. Jockeys wander around on the field in the distance. A boy just six chairs down from him is humming a song. The Power Company Building hums the song, too, but in the tone of electric current throughout the town, as in you could only hear it properly if your ears were adjusted to consider the pitch of the entire town's electrical supply all at once despite the distance between different tones happening in different kitchen appliances and wiring. All three of them, that is Sarah in her moment of working, Synesthesia in his moment of adjusting, and Kinesthesia in his moment of almost public dreaming (that being the kind of dreaming which is restless and makes the body move to re-enact the dream itself, tossing and turning around the bed), they almost hear it for a moment, that moment being the same simultaneous moment together, as if somehow all three and the Power Company Building are all singing together with only the head portion of the body and no disruption to the mouth. Mister Lonely does not know the song and cannot hear the song and continues circling before his trainer interrupts him and hands him over to the jockey who will race him, locking his body onto him using the legs. Sarah sits next to the hose and drinks water from it with her mouth, sucking it in.

She hears the announcements in the distance faintly, barely able to make out what is being said through the loudspeakers in the stadium. There is one last announcement to the gambling public: the race is about to commence. The jockeys are all ready on their horses in their booths before the shoot off. The gun goes, and the doors swing open. The horses run. The jockeys hit the horses to make them run faster, holding onto the reins. The sound is *of thunder*. The ground is beat up into a storm. Erosion follows the horses under the ground as fast it can, nearing those in the front of the race. The sun is low in the sky, nearing the tops of trees, turning everything a muted pink. People in the bleachers stand, as if standing will give them a better view. There's a big screen in the center of the track showing the race closer. The three horses near the front are Mister Lonely, Girl Winner, and Judith Come Home. The horses complete the first lap, and continue around for the second, and then the third and final lap, changing places as they go. Legwork. As they near the finishing point, the three horses in the front are Mister Lonely, Girl Winner, and Littlest Whorehouse In Texas. Judith Come Home is now fourth. All three front horses remain close, varying only slightly as they close in. True North grabs the hooves of Mister Lonely and he falls to the ground, only twenty feet before the finishing line. The jockey flies into the air and lands nine feet from the horse. This causes the other horses behind to panic, and the other jockeys try to move their way around the fallen horse as best they can without running over it or the jockey. Girl Winner crosses the finish line in first place, with Littlest Whorehouse in second, and Judith Come Home in third. There is a silence in the crowd. No one cheers over who won. They all wait impatiently as a medic runs out onto the track to help the jockey, crouching near him, while three other men come to help stabilize Mister Lonely. The medic helps the jockey to stand, and he gives a wave to the crowd as if to say that he is alright. The jockey is bleeding on his lower back and the back of his thighs and calves, and he is carried off the field. Synesthesia stares directly at True North, unknowing.

CONTINUOUS OPERATION

Kinesthesia blinks repetitively in an attempt to rediscover his vision, rubbing his eyes hard: What are my cards. You won, one of them admits, suddenly calm. Kinesthesia looks back up at them, seeing only blotches of red and orange. I'm going blind, he yelps, jumping up and knocking the table over. Thermal Energy and Continuous Operation are both sent hard onto the ground, their chairs and the table and the poker chips and the ash and the cigarette butts all crashing and colliding around them. Calm down! Continuous Operation shouts. Kinesthesia, in his delusion, runs out of the light, screaming. Thermal Energy pushes his chair off him, brushes away the ash, and stands, groaning, moving away from the reach of the ceiling light into the darkness of the rest of the room, following Kinesthesia. He gropes for his head in the dark and grabs him by the hair, pulling him close and back into the light, whispering to him bluntly to shut the fuck up. He says: I'll fix it you won don't worry I can fix it but only if you calm down. Kinesthesia stands as still as he can, panting hard, staring out at nothing, trying to overcome the panic. You're not blind, Thermal Energy assures him, putting both of his hands just slightly underneath Kinesthesia's t-shirt and running them slowly over the sides of his stomach. Continuous Operation pulls one of the chairs from its sideways position on the ground, puts it back the way it should be and helps Kinesthesia sit down. What do you mean, I can't see anything, he says. Put out your hand, Thermal Energy offers. Kinesthesia, unsure, puts out his hand and waits. They place an object in it. He can feel the texture and the shape—circular? glass? plastic?—and he can see in the darkness in front of him a blurred yellow light coming from his outstretched hand. And then his vision comes back to him, gradually. He blinks several times as this happens, adjusting his focus. He sees that he is holding a lightbulb and it is glowing, even though it is not screwed into anything. It's a gift, Thermal Energy says. Kinesthesia looks up at his face probingly. But it's not for you, Continuous Operation continues, it's for _____ (this being the place where the true name of Synesthesia would have been spoken, but since it is not documented in any way what his real name is, this will remain blank). What exactly am I supposed to do with it, Kinesthesia asks, now holding the lightbulb with both hands, examining it. He's been trying for months to get one, Continuous Operation explains. Thermal Energy adds: So he can test whether or not the energy is actually inside of him. But it's just a lightbulb and we have plenty of those, Kinesthesia says, confused: I mean anyone can go and get a lightbulb at the store, he steals money from his dad all of the time, he could get a lightbulb anywhere. It doesn't quite work like that, Thermal Energy says, standing behind him and holding his shoulders. He adds: But you have the ability to cure them—both of them—and we can help you.

BEFORE

Kinesthesia untangles himself from his sweat and bedsheets, trembling, and carries his half-clothed body from his bedroom, through the hallway, and into the bathroom. He flicks on the light switch and the florescent light above him goes on. He looks in the bathroom mirror. His hair is matted and wet to his skull, and his skin looks almost a pale green, which he attributes to both the lighting and the aftermath of dream. He puts his hand to his head to feel if he has a fever. He burns. He rummages through the drawers in the bathroom counter, and the cupboards below the sink, looking for a thermometer. He finds half-used band-aid boxes, old toothbrushes, wrappers, various medications, and then the thermometer buried underneath, which is a strip of plastic-like material kept in a small plastic case, with numbers on the bottom resembling a ruler. It is black. He takes it out of the case, places it on his head, and holds it there tight, waiting, staring at himself in the mirror. The thermometer strip starts turning red from zero upwards on the scale written on the bottom of it. It goes well past ninety-eight degrees and keeps rising. He throws it back into the drawer and then rummages for a bottle of aspirin, pops three pills into his mouth, turns the tap on, and ducks his head to it, sucking the water in and swallowing it, and then repeats this again, so that he has taken six pills. Synesthesia leaves the stadium and walks back to the stables to visit Sarah.

She is standing there, biting her hair, with an impatient look on her face. She is worried about the injured horse. He isn't drinking any water, she says. They both stand in the dark outside of his stable, mostly not saying words to one another, for a long time. Other Alterations puts its hands over both of their mouths during this until the hands sweat too much to leave them. Do you want me to stay, Synesthesia asks. She assures him that it's fine and he should go, but she is going to stay for the night. When they hug goodbye, he slips his losing ticket into the back pocket of her pants. Synesthesia takes off towards the highway. Kinesthesia takes a long bath in cold water before leaving his house for the night, wandering in the direction of the forest. The wind moves through the woods, and all the insects sleep soundly.

NORTH

One long recurring dream in the head of one falsely called Kinesthesia: the propaganda of North. In this dream, Sarah and Synesthesia are both there, standing in front of him, spaced out from one another. He realizes that the three of them are standing in a position that creates an equilateral triangle. Sarah's hair is in braids and she is holding her dress up over her face. Synesthesia has both of his hands on his face as if he is trying to cover as much of his skull skin as possible. None of them speak. Mister Lonely is also in the dream, behind Kinesthesia. The horse is on its back, not moving at all, legs in the air—as if from a video on pause. He doesn't see the horse. There is no sound at all in the room. Not even some white kind of noise. Both Sarah and Synesthesia reveal their faces and point in the direction of the horse. He turns around and sees Mister Lonely, and then looks back at them. Once he has turned around, they no longer have faces, and both of them are bleeding from the stomach. Kinesthesia turns around again and the horse is now frozen in mid-air, in a running pose. Both Sarah and Synesthesia are riding the horse together, also frozen. Neither of them is wearing clothes anymore. Their faces have returned, but they are completely expressionless. Kinesthesia notices that his stomach is bleeding, and he falls over, cradling himself. He tries to let out sounds of pain, but nothing comes. When he looks back, the room is entirely empty, and he is alone, surrounded by the blinding white. The only thing left in the room is a small piece of paper in front of him. He repositions himself on the floor so that he can pick it up and look at it. It's a ticket stub for a bet at the racetrack. The bet is on a horse named Mister Lonely for four dollars. Sarah appears behind him and grabs the ticket out of his hands and says: Hey, that's mine. Her mouth stays open on the last syllable of her speech and she freezes. A buzzing sound starts to come out of her mouth.

THE "IT" DISEASE

Four members of the Blue team find one another in one of the caverns created by the randomly placed rocks and broken bits of concrete, which are dispersed throughout the forest. They have an organized meeting about how one of them saw a group of Purples swimming near the edge of the water on the west side of the forest, trying to hide behind old harbours that have decomposed over time and are no longer in use. One of them asks if anyone has seen a Red or a Yellow and all of them answer that no, they have not, not for hours. They decide to do a sneak attack against the Purples if they are still where the one Blue member says he saw them. They crawl across the soil between the greenery hanging incandescent above them, all of this sunlight breaking through onto patches of their faces. They move like hunters: their only weapons being their ability to call out a name to someone else and spread the disease. Giving the name to someone else is the only way to cure the illness. Moving Water holds onto the Purples who are swimming and says: I will keep you safe but I must kill all of the horses and will you help me do it.

The Blues reach the edge of the forest to where it meets the water and duck behind the brush to look for the Purples in the swimming area with the harbour ruins. One Blue spots one Purple shirt which has been removed from a body, lying stranded on one of the rocks, which is sticking out of the water. That's cheating, he whispers to the others, pointing at it. Maybe we should call them It anyway since we see the colour, another one suggests. I don't think it works that way but now I have no idea what the rules are, says a third. The fourth current member of the Blue team doesn't say a word; he just stares out in wonderment at the water and the abandoned clothes.

One of them decides to remove his t-shirt, which is at the same time a removing of the identity. He sneaks slowly into the water around the rocks, nearer to the abandoned Purple shirt to check out the scene. The other members of his team wait in the brush for support. It should be mentioned that at this point, the Greens and the Oranges have almost given up on the game. Most of them are gathered in between a series of ruins on the beach, discussing together their lack of disease, whether or not anyone would even notice if they gave up on the game at this point in time.

The Blue gets close to the abandoned shirt and pulls himself up from the water onto the rock, looking around. The shirt doesn't seem to have an owner in sight. He looks back to his team, hiding in the brush, and makes a gesture that seems to say: I have no idea where they are. Moving Water looms around the Blue, standing there holding the Purple's shirt in his hands, looking distressed.

The Blue swims back to shore with the Purple shirt tied around his waist. The rest of his team emerges from the brush to greet him. I have no idea where they went but if we find some shirtless kid wandering around then we know who this belongs to, he says, shaking his body to get the water off of him as much as he can. The rest of his team agrees. Should we split up now, the quiet Blue asks. Yes: each of us in a direction, the somehow elected leader says. I'll stay near the water, one of them offers. Good, the leader responds. He then tells each boy, by pointing, to which direction they should run. The leader runs off in the direction of North, which is not True North.

The Purples are all split up throughout the woods. One of them is hiding underneath a canopy of fallen down trees, one of them is on the far side of the forest near the highway hiding in a bush, one of them has climbed half-way up a tree and fallen asleep, and another is wandering around shirtless in the open on one of the beaten down paths.

The leader of the Blue team wanders through a portion of the forest that is grown in, where no paths have been created, scarring up his knees and hands in the process. True North tries to redirect the Blue leader to him, whispering over and over: Eleven point three degrees. The magnetic energy of the earth agrees. But the Blue leader does not hear this.

The Blue that went east spots the group of Oranges and Greens sitting together on the beach. He yells: You're It! The group of boys all look in his direction, wondering which colour he means, but before he can explain, he darts back off into the woods. The boys sit for a moment and stare at one another, waiting for someone to speak and claim themselves as being It. I guess we should just rock-paper-scissors it, one of the Greens offers. Okay, an Orange agrees. Both boys shake their fists three times and say the name of the game: Rock, Paper, Scissors. The Green puts out a rock and the Orange puts out paper. Best two out of three? the Green asks. No way, the Orange says, and then all of the Oranges run off in different directions in the woods. It's getting dark, the Green says to his team. They all nod.

The leader of the Blue team, way off now in the direction of True North (another victory in the name of honesty) continues to trudge through the brush in the woods, no idea that he is no longer It, as is the same with the other three members of his team who were not witness to this moment of what will be known as *transference*.

TRUE NORTH

A compass held in the mouth region of the body between the teeth and tongue is similar to sticking a finger into a socket: electrifying. Hairs stand up on the body. This is not something to be alarmed about: it is just what happens. A map laid out on the table will tell you where to find North, but it will not tell you where to find True North. True North has a hiding place in dresser drawers, in the compass held in your mouth, and in the fires that happen only at night. Who would start a fire in the name of True North? Who would want to dim the artificial light and call out to the real light of the natural world? Is arson the light of the natural world? Is it natural to want to set fire to that technology you love so much, the one that's giving you light as you read your books blindly? Would you know how to read properly by the light of fire? Are the words different? Is your illiteracy less contagious, does it cause less of a genocide to the head portion of the body, can you closet your cancer calmly enough to wait for the words to ring out true to you? And there's that word again: True. What are you going to believe in, walking back and forth between these houses you've made?

NOW THEN

Three blind mice put the knives back in the barn. North is just a territory, briefly between breaths. If you do not consider how much sleeping could be done in the night, most of this is true. If you do not consider that fire is free if you put it in your mouth first or that there is feral energy being passed around, having conversations about trout, taking bananas from your kitchen, then night is quiet. But let's be honest. *This* night is not quiet. On this night, there is a fire, one carried in a human mouth from one place to another and set free. This particular fire is not swallowed in the night, during sleep. Yes: there is the possibility of transfer, of displacement, of movement. It is unlikely that a fire is coughed up accidentally, or made with the bare hands of someone young without thought, without purpose. It is true that this fire was made with much consideration, was stored in the mouth for weeks. Months. Years. Just waiting. Waiting and waiting and waiting to be wild.

OF MOVING WATER, EROSION AND OTHER ALTERATIONS

You are the very gold starfish. Could we
      grow each other
      back? I love you. You are
so bright, look at how much time we have spent in this
laundry machine (eternity? Infinite? Can god hear us
in here?) waiting to be dry, clean. All of our clothes, too.

The police left my house in the middle of the night. They took her and him with them. Him they brought home. Her they put in a bag. Him they gave back to beds. Her they made room for in the ground. I had to pick out the dress she would wear when it happened. All the rooms in my entire house were wet for weeks. The carpet was thicker. It had taken all of her blood. My father dragged himself around the house talking about how expensive the carpets had been. How long it had taken her to pick them out.

I wore her wedding dress to bed that night. Through the wall I could hear my father crying, which was something he never did. All the plants in the garden died from too much water. She drowned her garden, too.

At the funeral, my father wore white underwear underneath all the black. I saw him getting dressed in the morning. It was all I could think about for the entire day. I didn't own anything black so I had to buy it for the occasion. It was the middle of the summer. The funeral was outside. We all looked uncomfortable. My aunts cried until they conked out, their bellies full up of shrimp cocktails from the after party. My dad kept telling me not to call it that. A party, I mean. But that's basically what it was. The kind where only the adults are allowed to drink anything. I kept sneaking off to the bathroom to sit in the tub. I sucked water from the faucet, holding my hair back. If my father had noticed, I would have been scolded for it.

He was there with me. Holding my hand. Sweating. Licking his lips constantly to keep them from drying out. His parents came, too. His dad kept staring at me as if he wanted to say something really important. He kept quiet, though. Sucking all the words in.

we found her together.

the same one long note being held in the back of my head.
Which note is it, I wonder. No one will tell me. Droning on and
on. While he fucks me senseless. I hear it more than my own
breathing. Than his breathing. How do I tell him? Without singing
it? I am dizzy. He messed up some of the wires in me while he was
inside. I can't feel my arms a bit. My chest is heavy with yellow,
my ears a little burnt. I spit into his mouth as much as I can. I
leave my saliva on all parts of his body I can reach. It evaporates,
though. Dries out. It lifts from his skin and goes somewhere else.
The atmosphere? So parts of me are raining down on you in the
next town? On the other side of the world? I am moving across
the world in lifts of water? Even when most of it is frozen, when
most of the water I feel around me is snow actually coming down
my shoulders, in from the neckline of the worn out shirt, down the
chest. One long note coming out of me as water that is replanted
everywhere, systematically. One long note coming out of me as
electricity. Which shocks the water. I can't help but wonder
where the water must be going to. Where he goes at night. I have
followed him into blindness. There are other men pulling on his

arms sometimes. He has that pack of matches that I stole from my mother, just before. There is only one moment when I see his face in the dark. It's from the fire. Swallows the smoke. Passes it. Up against the trees, barking like dogs the whole time, the sound of the bark scratching his skin. The word bark. And what parts of his water are on

JanuXXy 9

I was thinking about jumping off the train bridge, too. He never asked me if I wanted to. It's too cold, now, he tells me, I have to wait for summer. But what would come of my body if I jumped in now. Would it break apart into separate islands of ice. If the water would be harder to hit. And what if I jump wrong and miss it, instead hitting the sky, completely free of my body. I put my arms in the water the other day at the lake until I couldn't feel them. Until they were almost ice. Just my arms and nothing else of me. Frozen stubs coming off my shoulders, that later, when they cooled, started to feel like they were burning and I didn't know how to stop it. I wanted to go swimming again but knew I could not do it. Looking at the distance across the river, I thought: it looks like it was made perfectly as the length for me to swim it. And even though the water now is bricks of ice shifting around, fish in one place for months filled with the last of their food, I think I could at least walk it, my legs could take it, I would be buoyant enough

65

and tough enough to channel it, yes and what kind of ice would I become if I wanted to do it, honestly, how do I get the fire going in me when it's so goddamned cold in this

MarcX XXX

XXXXX XXX xxX *to my room for a while to think about what I'd done, and I did just that. I thought about what I had done. She said: you are grounded young lady, because I did not want to put the dishes away in the cupboard tonight, because I did not want to eat all of the food on the plate. Her punishment for these things is nothing compared to the punishment I gave myself: leaving through the window, wandering out into the wild again. Meeting him that night, there, in the black, just far enough from the highway for the sound of cars to be almost clouded by the trees, just close enough to the Power Company Building to have my head full of noise—and for what? The difference between her and him is the method of punishment, the way of showing just how much one cares. If I cradled his head in my hands long enough, he would start to whimper and his mouth would open suddenly with so many words, and I would hear nothing except the energy, and his head would fill up with spit and sand coming out into my hands, onto my lap. The only way to put a stop to it is to undress, and as I do so she scolds me somehow. And the trees here seem to be singing but I don't recognize*

Dear _____,

I thought about telling you a secret. I think I leave a lot of them in your room. Anyway, I wanted to tell you that I had this dream that you were the father of my child, and you were a very good father, but I was a bad mother. In fact,XXXXX
XX XXX xXXXXXXXX xX

SeXXXmbXr

It was you. Sleeping in my garden. Not throwing rocks at my window. What were you waiting for? For me to sleep? I will not do it. Not now or ever again. It's all his fault anyway—it's really him you shoulXXXXXX

July 9

What's been happening is the sirens blaring and this lack of light everywhere and my dad hiding in the storm cellar. It's like everyone went mute, like as if without the TV they can't talk, as if without the light they don't know what dark is. I've been sleeping in the ash most nights since. I cannot stand to be in the stables. And I just keep singing these songs because I have to have something

to do with my mouth without him I have to have something to do
with this mouth goddamn it

June 3 Xxx6

having been in her shoes, her dressing gowns, her body
shaped into the bed: somXXXXXX my father clung to this one
photograph in particular, and I rememXxxXXXXXXX and no
one touches me I am a

I choked through mornings, passing cigarettes between my hands and his. I watched him pull the smoke inside, not knowing how much of it he kept contained. If I was the one strangling him, or him me, or him him. The trucks on the highway were blaring off and on as they passed. I would walk along the highway to get to the racetrack. I would work with the newborn foals, trying to get them to walk.

He would ask me about the horses. Who was winning, who was losing. He was keeping tabs of it in his head, maybe, for later gambling. I walked barefoot around the barns because I wanted straw scratches on me. He would have my feet against him and ask about the marks. I would say: Horses.

I would pull his feet against me and ask about the marks. He would say: North.

I removed my shirt in front of him and showed him my chest. I'm changing, I said. He looked at my chest and didn't say anything. I grabbed him by the wrists, slowly, and pulled his arms up to me. I made him touch me where I was changing. His hands were sweating at first, but they seemed to dry out the longer he was in contact with me. I let go of his wrists but his hands stayed there, getting heavier, just where I had placed them. I reached down towards his pants and fumbled with the button and the zipper for a moment before pulling them open, and pulling him out. You're getting bigger too, I said. He got thicker in my hands. He leaned in and whispered to me: Blood. It's all blood

I'm filled with. I leaned closer to him also and replied: Water. We're mostly water.

I had to hide the bloodstains on the bed from my mother and father. I did not want them to see what was coming out of me. I kept putting more and more pillows on my bed to cover it up. They were fresh and white. I could still smell it, though. What had come out of me and what had come out of him. It was stale on the sheets no matter how many times I washed them.

He would run off to the bathroom immediately after to remove the latex that we had between us. And every so often I could hear him throwing up, and I would ask him. He would say: I am sick and the doctors can't seem to figure out why.

There were two boys strangling one another in my stomach. My mother was in the bathtub, watching all three of us. The most beautiful sound was this noise in me. Coming out of my head at night.

I tried to tell him about this. I said: Songs. He said: Energy. We said: Horses. We said: Sleep.

He was heaving, once, in the backyard, leaving all of my mother's dinner in the flowerbed. Immediately after, he mentioned something like: he didn't know how to get it out of me. And I asked him if the porkchops were that bad. He grimaced and turned away, throwing up again, contorted over the lilies.

The police didn't find me and take me home. I thought they would. I would stay in the parking lot for extended periods of time shivering from the lake, my clothes still wet. Before my braces were removed, I thought maybe the energy was just my teeth being held too tight. My jaw was always sore.

I wanted him to know about it. I told him: it's the Power Company Building. He had never really been there, even though it was where his dad worked. He said his dad didn't ever really talk about it, his job. So I took him. We rode there on our bikes. I made sure we did it at night because I didn't want to get caught.

The building itself wasn't necessarily large, but it felt as much. We would sit there, in the parking lot, both feeling the energy. Kissing, trading saliva, holding hands. It was a completely different experience to be there with him, with someone else who could feel it. I didn't want to do anything else, but he said his stomach was bothering him. We biked back together. I dropped him off at his house and went home.

A routine formed from this. A pattern of long nights, perpetuating themselves. We stopped being able to count on our hands how many times a day we were going. Any time we could sneak away long enough. He seemed happier, at first. Took more of an interest, spoke more, touched more. But then the skin around his eyes got blacker. It was sudden. He slept less, talked less. Missed classes all of the time. When I looked at him I wasn't sure who I was looking at. This strangled head on a body barely walking around.

The sound of the energy wasn't really enough to overcome it. I could still hear her louder than anything else. In the woods at night, all I could hear was her voice, running at me like horses. It wasn't even that there was music coming out of all of the rooms. It was that parts of it were inside me, too. If I could crack my ribs open, I imagined I would find pipe organs. That my inner body was a cathedral of instruments, an orchestra of one. The energy really was just a means of playing these organs before I got my head around music theory. When I finally learned how to sing me, I was then accompanied by the energy. We worked as a team to make the sound. We sang holy, we coerced traffic to halt, my ribcage got bruised, and my throat went wild, howling. *Hum.*

Horses Running 07/07/97 6:45PM $4(*handwritten*)

Judith Come Home
Girl Winner
Mister Lonely   ( )
Littlest Whorehouse In Texas
Emperor Of Rome
Grand
A Hard Rain's A-Gonna Fall
Viva Las Vegas
East Wood
Kickin Up Some Ruckus

There was a group of them that gathered in the park to sing. We had heard them. The songs, that is. We knew them, too. They were branded in us. But something in the energy blocked them from us, made us to forget. Selective memory, I guess. We wanted to learn how to make the sound ourselves. That low hum.

The treehouse, for example, was created almost as an attempt to build our own Power Company Building. It was a nucleus of electricity that we had made with our own hands. Wires, cords, plugs, lamps—we collected these. They all sang to us a song more vivid than I'd ever heard a human mouth make. They purred perfect notes in harmony with one another. A fifteen-lamp symphony.

For a long time, only large amounts of the energy at once were enough to dull the sounds in my head. Even if only slightly.

We tore the treehouse down eventually. We knew it wasn't our place. We couldn't create the sound with our mouths or any other parts of us because we were still human, not machines. Although the energy had chosen us as a vessel of some kind, as a place to be harboured, we could not necessarily find a way to communicate this verbally. We even gave what was left of our treehouse to the Power Company Building as a peace offering. That was his idea, not mine.

I had been slowly getting rid of the secrets that I had been hiding, all these little pieces of my life that I thought I wanted to keep in boxes, as old paper, as photographs, still moments. The fire sped this process up—I was leaving it all over town as fast as I possibly could. Drowning them in the lake, even.

I stood on the dock staring out at the rowboat, which had drifted out into the lake. As if someone had taken it out to drown themselves. Shivers spread along the hair on the parts of my legs I missed shaving. I thought about how much weight I would need on me to sink. How would the water take me; would I go easy.

The police sirens were still going off. They sounded like church bells, far away. Singing: dull and dragging. It was the energy that I'd heard in the mornings before. In the seashell cadence. I gave them seashells so that they could hear the sound and they swapped them back and forth. He was handling me through my shirt, droned out. A room for piano, vacant. I saw them pushing themselves together even though it wasn't really made to fit. And me in the corner with the seashells, waiting for them to recognize me. They seemed to be having trouble conjuring up a relationship with me. Both unable to speak, or breathe, even. *And a rock feels no pain. And an island never cries.*

This morning there was no energy. Only sirens, the dull light of the sun just rising, casting a dusk on me. The water turning a cold yellow around my ankles. My legs knocking against the dock. The rowboat moving further away into the distance.

The water was warm. More so than ever. Like: *burned.* As if it could be. *Scorched.* And the birds overhead were all moving erratically like they had no idea where they were supposed to be, their sense of direction thrown off by the smoke that slowly filled the sky, and I unraveled the ball of twine I had with me, tying rocks around my ankles, this lovesong coming out of my mouth like a plague.

Since then horses were sea salt in my arms. A mare is a horse that is a mother. I had a mother and she had a death. I was a mother for a moment when I took care of him. He was my son. But I never gave birth because we put latex between us. We protected ourselves from the problem of children. He said: Children don't have children. I asked him: Don't I have you?

My first real blood started when I stopped singing. He helped me clean it up with paper towels. I didn't tell my father. My father was a horse that could not swim. He did not know very much about blood. My mother took me to the drug store and we got the right things to take care of it.

I snuck a pack of condoms into my coat pocket. I said: No mothers today, tomorrow. No children. I did not have foals coming out of me for the sake of it.

We all agreed on this.

A death is my mother, her body cleaned out of organs and put into the ground. A child is my father feeling the need to cry over it. A child is a son that is abandoned by the mother, a daughter being fucked by boys in the other room.

Horses carry all of us into heaven after we die. In heaven I am the mother of horses.

THE POWER IS OUT, SING

We spent the Sabbath in bathtubs trying to get clean not spending any money. I decorated the walls of my bedroom with leftover tinfoil from lunches, and when I walked to school, I could hear change moving in my pocket against my thigh. I gave him thunder from under my shirt. He kept it, then, under his.

By diffusing the lightbulbs in the attic we were able to forget our age, all of our identification lost in smells. The light from the window, the energy creeping in through the floorboards. And when we sat and looked through those boxes of who we used to be, we were there again. And it was impossible to forget who we were before fucking, before reels of tape on the kitchen counter, hidden in the attic walls. Before all of the blood on the mattresses, tracing trails through the forests for me to find him with other men. In the house during the winter, I could imagine different shadows against the wood, paint peeling from around the bathroom sink, all the rust in our mouths. The texture of her sandals falling away from her toes. By putting my tongue against it, I memorized the grain of phrases, the knots in the bark wrapped around our ankles. I sweat through the night thinking about the garden, all of the weeds pulled out with the daffodils, the hose left running into the grass. I kept these things inside of myself. I did not have a hiding place anywhere else. I knew everything with my sore stomach and that was enough for me.

We made a house out of snow that we lived in for a while, the three of us, but never all three at the same time. Sarah said she didn't need heat. I prefer ice, she said. I held out my appendix in her general direction and asked her to set it on fire. I prefer fire, I said.

He dug a hole in the center of the snow house that he hid extra blankets in. In the spring, the house melted and all that was left in the yard were scarves and sticks, we moved back into yellow drywall rooms. The three of us but never all three at the same time.

I took my bike to look for him in the ashes, slumped in the remains of the Power Company Building. He had a map of Alaska. He said: One day I will be everywhere. His arms and cheeks were black as he said this. I avoided looking at the map directly. He had his ear to the pavement of the highway. The quiet is too heavy, I can't hear anything, he said, his whole head filled with blankets. I lay on the ground with him and put my ear against the cement and heard nothing, too.

Too many gears and not enough volume.

I asked him if he had measured his length, and he said: No. I asked him why not, and he said: It's just skin. I told him I had been measuring my own and that in the past year it had grown over an inch. He pointed at the river and said: It will never be as long as a river, the distance between one land mass and another. I thought aloud: Maybe a small brook or creek? He looked at me, clean, and told me that what was between his legs was just broken branches and sticks, kindling for campfires; it would never be the length of any body of water.

The thing is that he was not the kind of person to name birds or ask about what colour you thought the sky was. He scattered his diction in variation, he said: Let's fuck each other back into solids, I want to be solid. He preferred what came easy, what he could control. He would readily admit things like, *I'm scared shitless*, but he would never fill in the blanks.

I was very direct looking at him and said (pulling his body): You are solid, these are your bones. He pulled away skeptically, disrupting the bedsheets.

He would ask me about the stomach ache and I would say: Yes, there is this metal sitting inside of me, I think my stomach is going blind. The bed would stay the way it was, pillowcases covered in crusts of us, leaks that were transitory, and he would say: I can cure it, just fuck me back into solids, we'll do it to one another and there won't be any pain anymore.

He drained all of the sweat from my skin, jutting between the grass and the thorns, waving his arms wild. He left bruises on my back holding me inside him, like I would never return.

I asked him: How come we have everything. His hair was lengths cut into meat, arranged neatly around his face. He would tell me: I am proud of every mark I've made on you. Assuming they were all his. I was proud of them, too. The marks on me and the marks that I had given him in return, though I knew that most of his were collected from other men.

I asked him: How can I pull things out of you and I don't mean my cock. All I wanted was to draw out the noise from his head. To sonata him somehow. To make more out of his language, somehow. But he just said it again, *I'm scared shitless*, and he didn't ask what I meant, pulling the matches from the cupboards, looking for glasses of water.

Sarah carried the empty dresser drawer down Thompson Road, dragging it across the cement, singing 'I Am a Rock' with one hand in the pocket of her paisley dress, one that she stole from her mother's closet. She said she was slowly trying to empty her room, that her head was crowded enough.

Why do they call them bodies of water, she asked me, throwing her sandals into the lake. I wanted every fault in her feet, but I sat still in wet sand and traced 'you are' into it, because it was true, although I was unsure of how to say it with my mouth. My body is water, she said, all this caging for what would be lakes.

I thought about how much water I had given her, how she had dried out all my skin into blisters, and imagined the shape she would be if she were a lake. If I were a river. If I could feed her until she could flood.

We tried to make a campfire in the boy's room, but we ran out of kindling. We watched the horses from the window and wrote our names side by side on the bathroom stall.

I can't remember my favourite colour, I told him.

You have time, he lied.

I tried to look into the light to find my favourite colour, but all I saw was this amount of liquid, that amount of fire. This amount of skin from me, which I gave to him, as a late birthday present. As in: I didn't remember when his birthday was. It could have been at any time.

Sarah's arms were longer than the Mississippi river. I found this out in my seventh grade geography class. I wanted to measure them while she was sleeping, but the spider plants in her house talked away the night, gnawing it down to every little last hair on her. She left all of the doors open on her house, waiting for the spider plants to vacate themselves. She said she couldn't lose any more sleep. They had been there for over ten years, and she kept her mouth shut the entire time, listening intently to everything they had to say, wide awake with the comforters pulled up around her neck, like she was only a head coming out of a body of snow.

In the hallway leading to her room, there was a photograph of her at the age of seven, her mouth full of metal. She said it was worth it for perfect white fences, her tucked teeth. We shared a ginger ale, and I pissed next to the shed in her backyard. She said: Look now you've left your mark you'll always be there. I hucked antibiotics from my thighs, and she tried to point out north to me again. I pulled my pants back up and covered my eyes.

The doctor put the stethoscope to my heart and counted how many times it beat in one minute. I asked her to tell me how many times and she gave me a number that I don't remember. She asked if I was still throwing up in the mornings and I said: Yes, fire. How many hours approximately are there between your last meal and the time you go to bed, she asked. I told her that it varies. Approximately, she repeated. An hour or two, I said. She requested that I wait at least five hours between my last meal and my bedtime and see if that changes anything, and that I should avoid spicy food. I told her that I do not eat spicy food, just fire while I am sleeping. She put her hand on my forehead, like she was checking for a fever in me, and asked if I'm at least taking my pills and are they helping out during the day. I lied to her and told her that they were.

I don't remember much about the day the Power Company Building burned down. I was in the stables, the horses all looked like they were losing water. I spent the night by the highway counting cars but could not feel the energy anymore. I listened to the police sirens in the distance instead, the only noise that kept my head open, picturing the kind of light a fire that big would produce. If it could swallow the enormous black of the sky, of our burnt bones.

He told me that he needed more than just plans, that there was so much heat rising from the river. He was tired of jumping off the train bridge, of riding our bikes as far as we could only to find more fields, more empty space. He said: We should set fire to the farmhouses, I want to know what smoke tastes like, why are you wasting all your money on girls and horses, why are all the books we own autobiographies.

He carried a library around with him in his head and I thought about what letters existed between Z and A—a secret alphabet between the one that we used in our speaking with one another. I figured he just needed a good clean reminder: a campfire, a forced fuck, a lesson in heat.

We exhausted our nights in the parking lot of the local grocery gluing Xeroxed paper that said THE MAP IS NOT THE TERRITORY to the bricks of bank buildings. His eyes were three different colours. He said he hadn't been drinking, there was just so much wood, so much length, not knowing where to put his vertigo. I said: My pockets are empty, I have nothing for you.

I'll fill them with smoke, he said. That's all I need.

We went to the truck stop later, because he said he needed something to wait for. I watched him look at all the men as they came through, complaining to the waitresses about their wives and weather. I don't remember what I put in my coffee.

Sarah was a pantry worker—she did not keep clothes anywhere but drawers, she did not have closets of corduroy. Her bed was littered with pillows, endlessly arching over the mattress and falling onto the floor. There were all of these little things about her that she would never admit to me. Maternal instinct is easy, she said, I want more. We tore our treehouse down in parts, selective about what nails to pull out, where to put them. It filled time, not rooms—we left all of the wood near the Power Company Building, all planks like bare bones, untended.

What horses were running that day is hard to say. Sarah tended to shift involuntarily between the stables, she knew all of their names better than I could ever remember. I do not know anything about feed, if only there were bread, and if only I could sew it straight on. She moved back and forth between horses, filling buckets up with water and hoisting them around. I was busy memorizing her leg muscles.

I turned to her and said: I think I forgot the Lord's Prayer. She stared at me with what looked like a fever. Before returning to the barn she said: I cannot fix you.

The organic parts of her looked like they had been dug out of the leftovers of old horses. The ones that couldn't run anymore. She called me a hunter and said I was hunting for secrets. I touched the three scars on me underneath my t-shirt and thought about the noise we made between rooms and if anyone else could hear it. If what we left behind us could ever be found without a good clear map. The map I didn't want to see, the one she kept on her body, all while she tried to balance glasses of milk on her head, the sound of guns in my gut in the dark of her bedroom.

All the horses I bet on lost. I borrowed her clothes without telling her, later trying to stuff them back into drawers the way they were, this sweater over that one, still smelling of vinegar, like I could never fit into them in the first place.

He had navigated the woods long enough to know all the best spots. He liked being out in the open. He said: We're sharing something bigger this way. This swaggering and swinging of these bodies between these briars with all the eyes of night watching. The sun closing its eyes, and mine tight, too. Picking ticks off of my legs after.

I had an orgasm in the mouth of three hundred whales, which were all him, and which were all her. This is easy to describe if I use my hands to tell the story. In the story, he is the whale that ate Gappetto and she is the whale that ate me. Both of them ate the rivers, the fires, the storms.

On one hand, we had mattresses ready for us. On the other, there was the soil around that could be gardened, planted, produced with. The ground had children and we had shelter, good homes, food in our mouths when we needed food in our mouths.

He brought a bag filled with wires and cords. I brought most of my dad's magazines, which he hid in the wall of his closet with his other secrets. The magazines had photographs of girls in them mostly, but after a while of looking I couldn't tell the difference anymore. All I saw in them was skin. It could have belonged to anybody.

When we were pulling our clothes back on, I tore up the map of Alaska while he was still working on his pants. He didn't ask me why I did it. All of the reasons were large tumors protruding from my skull. Antlers and long branches of trees. I still saw pieces of the earth encrypted onto the paper, but now it was too fragmented for me to know where we were, or what direction we were going in. He stood—clothed, covered in charcoal—and took the torn pieces of the map from me, putting them in his pocket. Don't worry, he assured, I'll make sure you never find it.

My father was killing sharks in his sleep. He would howl at night, grinding his teeth, trying to swim, attack, pull them apart before they did it to him. My mother was unaware of this. She slept like a log on the far side of their king-sized bed, right along the edge. Never moving. Looking more like a newly dead body than a sleeping woman.

He worked pretty regular shifts at the Power Company Building. Nine to five. He didn't talk about his job. When he got home, my mother would make dinner, and he would sit at the table in the dining room and wait staring at his bare plate. He looked like he was fighting a stroke most of the time and didn't say anything during dinner unless asked a question, to which he would answer as briefly as possible, if at all.

After dinner, my father did dishes before retreating to his room for the rest of the night with the door closed. My mother spent this time organizing the pantry, counting and cataloguing all of its contents, keeping a relentlessly updated list on the refrigerator of all of the things we needed. When my father resurfaced from his room, he would spend the rest of his awake hours gleaming, smiling, eyes welled up with water and glazed green. My mother never noticed this.

Some nights, I would sit outside of my parent's bedroom and put my ear to the door after my father had gone in there alone. There was the stuck static of singing somewhere else. The buzz of what I remembered as *music*. But indistinct. As in:

I heard *hum* and I heard *buzz* and I heard *please, leave the lights on*, all the appliances in the houses singing, too.

My parents only seemed to have one thing in common that was discussed out loud, and that was the electric bill. They turned the lights off as frequently as possible. I was patronized almost daily for leaving lights on in rooms—to the point where, if I left my bedroom to use the bathroom for a few minutes, I would come back to find my room dark, the lights switched off, followed by a long lecture about wasting electricity, and how using more of it doesn't increase dad's pay any, and haven't we had this talk before already. I said: Yes, okay, I'm sorry, I won't do it again. One of the things that my mother catalogued very well was the amount of lightbulbs in the house. I swear she kept track of how long they lasted, too.

The blackout was a huge relief on him; I think he was trying to escape it. He seemed more than happy to walk around the house numb all hours of the night in the darkness, with nothing to do and no reason to go to sleep or get up in the morning. My mother lit as many candles as she could, and the house stunk of vanilla and gasoline. We ran out of firewood on the third day. After that, we burned books.

SYNESTHESIA

.

One of the horses died the night of the fire.

The negative charge of water is due to unshared pairs of electrons. Fire can sustain its own heat. Both argue about who is going to do the dishes. Both swallow oxygen. They steal it from your body, over time. You will run out of the house gasping for air because they took all of what you could have had in you. If you wait long enough, you will notice how much your skin has been burnt by the sun and how much of your body is water. If you rub yourself against wood long enough, you will spark. In the forest, there are trees split by the sound of thunder, leftover wood waiting to be burned. All bodies of water are filled, somehow, with flesh. You say we will run out if we leave the taps running, but it is coming back to us. Coming out of our ears, even.

A challenge is presented: how did one body break into three, how did they come from so many different mothers everywhere in rooms undressed, how do you shove them all back into each other simultaneously without breaking the skin, is it important to leave the skin intact, are all objects made up of smaller objects, and how do you know where they meet and fit together if they are always moving. A father stands between two electric wires and it changes the fluid that comes out of him later. It breaks apart into three.

Most of the silos have no lights inside them. If you enter them at night and look up, it takes a long time for your eyes to adjust, for you to see that above you is circular and closing in. There are tape recordings of you in the silo slowly realizing this. There is a box in her attic filled with tape recordings of energy that no one has ever heard.

A fire door is the only kind of exit you should take when leaving a building. Remember: a building could always be on fire.

.

The seabed is overflowing with nickel, metal produce, fillings for cavities. A singer who can hit the highest note is looking directly out of a window, facing the ocean, facing true north. The note she is singing produces what is known as *magnetic energy* in the earth. If you attempt to swallow a compass to guide you to true north, the compass will sit in your belly, inert for many years. The magnetic energy beneath the rock of the earth is in constant flux. As in: it is digesting. As in: it just had its last good meal. All movement in the earth is, of course, very slow. The ability to move around without knowing your destination is easily taken for granted. As in: *drifting*. You may wake up some mornings with sores in your mouth. Rust, too. If you stand facing north, the north that you probably believe in, and tilt your body only slightly at an angle (that being both to the side and forwards), you will be staring true north directly in the face. And what is it telling you? How to get home, how to kill your pet, how to make it look like it was anyone's fault but your own. Exactly what you've been waiting all this time to hear. The truth is that the magnetic energy of the earth has control over your blood. It wants you foaming at the mouth. It wants you home at midnight, no later. If you listen too long, your body will revolt. It may sound funny now, but you will wake up one day sick, throwing up compasses for no good reason, asking the doctor why there are fires in your stomach, burning your mouth good in the night, making it impossible to eat or keep down your food, apologizing to your mother that your dinner's gone cold because you couldn't finish it, and all this time still beneath your feet the earth is moving, shifting, re-arranging the furniture without asking you where the hell you wanted the sofa.

A girl and a boy and a boy and a river. All speaking the same language, congruently, but forgetting how to return the favour. A girl standing in the river trying to swim it and tame it. A boy trying to tame a boy in the river trying to tame it. A boy following the river currents currently and incorrectly. And a river not speaking. If one person is quiet long enough, someone else around them might speak. If this is true, then there must always be a person in shock raving about last night's dinner. Look at the facts: a girl made the dinner. A boy was in the stables when the dinner was being prepared. A boy was wondering what to eat for dinner. A river ate all of them. A river never stops raving.

The horse's death was not investigated, mostly because all investigative energy was spent on figuring out who started the fire.

The heat capacity of water is the second highest of any known chemical compound. Ammonia is first. Ammonia is taking the money instead. Ammonia wants to hug you like it is casual and okay for you to do so because you are the good kind of friends who hug casually when you see one another. It is important to know that Ammonia is just distracting you so that water will get lukewarm and finally, freeze. The transformation between water and ice is similar to that which happens to a person when they fall asleep at night. Ice is a solid, hovering over the lake floor, hibernating. If water is most of you then you can become solid, too, at the right temperature. If water were watching over us, directing storms which way to go, they would bring them all here immediately, no questions asked.

Some schools of atoms orbit the springs fresh with sex. They buzz together like a group of hungry flies inside of a dead animal's mouth or head: in unison, all ringing, genderless, rubbing their lack of pronouns on one another's lack of genitalia. Somewhat for warmth, mostly for friction. Yes: they are always moving, you knew this. And they have made you, moving constantly, a solid, these many little pieces of worn weight. Spinning their magnetic moments, they spew the whole story out for you: Yes, they all came from me and you, from carp's blood, from the daughters of electron pairs in dance halls everywhere, three of them from no one's belly, from between the legs of someone who had nothing there but match burns and a colostomy bag, hallelujah, a miracle birth.

You can tell them that there are dogs tearing apart your yard, all through the night while you are asleep. You can say whatever you want to say, if it helps you. But the truth is there are children tearing apart your yard, all during the day, and you are letting them do it. You are watching them from the front window. Your own children behaving like animals. Your own children, which came out of you, which you made with more than your hands, are sharpening their teeth on the tennis courts. They are hiding and seeking. All of them are murderers, but you don't need to say anything about it. As long as you keep the grass cut and tend to your garden at every spare moment. As long as your neighbour still says to you around dinner time every day: how do you keep your yard so magnificent, where did you get so many good seeds.

It is important to know that in the case of an electrical fire, the water is conductive to the electricity and will only help the fire to spread.

A list, so you do not forget:

1. Those tiny little pieces that make up you and me, that keep our clothes on, that keep us solid even though they are moving, always moving, these little pieces are you and are me and are us.

2. How, at times, this cannot be communicated between us, how there are parts of it that are not expressed verbally: reaction times, sensations, non-auditory revelations, nervous systems twitching. Mouths not speaking. A ringing in the wind, perhaps.

3. The way we discuss that which we are experiencing with some form of language, the level of intimacy that exists between us while we have this conversation, the depth of understanding, the amount of words that we could use to describe all of the parts, how we sense them, how we react, what is even motivating us to move at all.

What is left is known as *evidence*, but certain texts on this subject have been lost. For example: all three birth certificates have been lost. A boy and a girl and a boy. An individual, left unidentified, can be dangerous. Three is worse. Not having any kind of documentation to prove that you exist basically means that you do not. Exist. You never did. Where did you come from. Get out of my kitchen.

The horse didn't have a funeral. Horses don't have funerals.

Some of the flames that lick the endless edges of the roof of your mouth were unwanted, sure. They call it what it is: a wild fire. A wildfire. It didn't ask anyone for permission to be placed in the nursing homes. In the lofts of barns full of kindling. Crawling, crowning, and jumping from roof of mouth to roof of house to tops of trees to bottoms of meat, across the ground, into old pits that used to be its home. Cooking what needed to be cooked and could not be cooked by any one particular individual. No one planned on this, or so they say. This kindling was not left out in the servitude of *fire*. For some singular amount of natural warmth to come over them and, unabridged, undefeated, cross them over with ginger smolder, choke them to death with black smoke, thick, you sighing away from it, you beating the ground with your fists. Keep sleeping, even if you see them. Only you can prevent forest fires? They started of their own accord and they were meant to happen. What did you want? You wanted wild. You are.

Your parent cells are swimming the deepest ocean looking for the perfect house. A house underwater is difficult to maintain due to certain amounts of pressure on the walls and pillars holding the structure of the house in place. Depending on how far down your parents decide to live, also, electricity becomes more expensive, because at a certain depth there is no more natural light, which of course means running the lamps longer. You are too preoccupied to notice this because you have not been born yet, you have not been made a good daughter cell. Your parents have slept through binaries and have tried to furnish one hundred empty rooms for you, limp-wrist zygotes, screaming as you appear as if from nowhere in hospital beds, onto the floor. This multiple birth process is eventually confusing because your mother starts to forget which child you are and you are orphaned back into the ocean. There are only so many children she can take care of. Your fraternal brothers and sisters cannot follow you. A family cannot stay together in this situation. Fertilization has not yet been governed by the great sea. You are only one small part of this process, and you must fend yourself. Your brothers and sisters will certainly try to find you, to put your bodies back together again, but you cannot let them. Who are they anyway? Do you know? If you were to even want to call out their names, which in the water is difficult to do as the sound is denser, would you know what to call them?

In a math class, there are three students: A, B, and C. A asks *isosceles triangle* and the teacher answers *two equal sides.* B asks *equilateral triangle* and the teacher answers *all equal sides.* C asks *scalene triangle* and the teacher answers *no equal sides.* This is how facts are arranged in a classroom setting. Some children have carved triangles into their bones knowing which kind of triangle is perfect for them, branding into them immediately their interactions with others from then on in their lives. The tattoo is a way of avoiding a simple human pain: *change.* The triangle is secure and can always be relied on. If you stay inside this house then you will always be okay and you will never have to die, either.

There are other ways, and I allude here to penetration of different parts of the body with another, mostly, to share warmth without actual visual damage to your person. Violence is in our nature though, right? We are willing to pollinate anything.

Yet we have been drawing the world on paper for a long time. First, it was just how to get to the liquor store from here where I am: yes, standing at this point, how would I get there. But the liquor store just kept getting further and further away, verbal instructions no longer being enough. So we put trails on paper. As in: the paths normally taken. We cut up trees and flattened them the way we had done for our journals, our history, which we record in what we called a *language* with what we called our *hands* almost stuck to the table. The sickness as first located in the human stomach by a league of serious doctors and scientists who were also at the time studying the magnetic energy of the earth. See: there were magnets poisoning all of the villagers. They were in the tap water. The villagers were plagued with them, running around screaming: How do we get somewhere anywhere. Thus: medical attention. Thus: north, south, east, west. Lawyers responsible for the neverending question of who is right and who is wrong about direction. The compasses of the world all listening to liars. As if you couldn't tell from the sun, from the stars, from the way all things in the living sky were speaking simultaneously, saying: Go this way, go that. And maps: our way of containing the world around us so we can hold it in our hands and point to where we live and say: Look, it is here, this is my location, I have never had another one, I barely know where I've been.

The heirloom is inserted directly into the mouth during sleep: it is tradition. Through the cortex. Through the tying down of the hands and the feet. One family member must stand in a hallway in the crossfire of stereo sound, and the rest of the family is in separate rooms, gliding between the hallways, trying to court them to dance. The music that is played is sometimes referred to as *transition music*. A father can make an heirloom from any part of his body. It will carry on the disease involuntarily. Some family members like to take photographs of this occasion, while others prefer only to close their eyes at night and remember it how they'd like to remember it.

A horse's hooves and hides are in your house, flooding the libraries, holding the books together, they couldn't run anymore, they fell right over in the middle of a race for no reason, and we have found a way to put almost anything we can to good use.

Water is working turbines by turning them with force. Force is water moving through machines to make them work. Work is the action of digging up your mother from her grave and putting her back in the room that she died in. The room that she died in may no longer exist, and if this is the case, please call the police immediately for reconstruction. A reconstruction is the bombing of an area with nuclear weapons. A nuclear weapon is the sweet body of a young thing having its first and foremost. The first and foremost is a good fire, a hot bed of coals. A is before B which is before C, which is known as chronology. *This happened* and then *this happened*. This is why one might be known to keep the lights on: to see that which unfolds before them.

One egg fertilized by how many sperm—count them, can you? The eggs can multiply, too. Think of the endless possibilities of production that can be going on inside of you. If you are pulling polar body twins from the receptacle of the living womb, that great wide wall of open tissue, there is always going to be more pulling than you could ever even imagine. Chimeras are wandering around with pieces of their mother, their sisters, their brothers, and sharing them with strangers, inviting them in for more implantation, eventually a baby has to get sick, eventually one of them has to come out of you only as a liquid and not as a solid, and you can cry and sob about it all you need to, but there are children walking around everywhere without arms, without pieces of their mothers, their sisters, their brothers, and sharing only what they do have of themselves with strangers. And you can count the eggs, the sperm; you can't do it on just your fingers, your toes. The sonogram will show you what you have been growing for so long. Three twins. Triplets. And will they come out of you proper, will you scream at the doctor the entire time, will you want the whole world to see what they have done to you, passing through the rooms of strangers?

A good doctor can sterilize all of the leftovers inside you, trust them. Their job is to delay your death for as long as possible.

There are deposits of their semen in the church pews and all over the good book. God's children are good children, and they never do anything wrong. They never leave traces of themselves on anything. After they die the only way you can tell they were there in the first place is by looking at the yard sale section of the newspaper.

Water has an addiction to being in the lungs, this we know, and children are the easiest targets in water. Your children are drowning. Swimming culture doesn't want you to know the truth, but there is a high possibility that you could drown immediately when near water at any given time. This means, if you are afraid to die, then stop doing the dishes, showering, watering the plants, drinking, pissing, bleeding. But let's face it: your own body is mostly water, and therefore you could drown unwillingly at any time. Even if you survive the initial calamity, there are cases of secondary drowning, during which the chemical changes in your body from the near drowning experience will cause your death anyway. Swimming and dying are therefore essential, walking hand in hand, so whenever you're ready, the water is nice.

The depersonalized individual cannot tell the difference between the way the hands slide against the skin and the way that they hear the sound of sparks as if from nowhere. They walk around feeling as if their body is being lifted constantly by the weight of the air on the eyes, internalizing the world around them as fragments, letting dogs bite them, sleeping in rain storms for warmth, cutting off all of the human hair of the head to taste again. And not knowing a single song. And not knowing a single true thing. But what is it to know through the body, anyway, what is it to trust it, this knowing.

Malleus, Incus, and Stapes are all sitting in a room. They are laughing at you. There is a labyrinth inside of your head filled with primary colours, semicircular canals where you think you are hearing odd numbers being shouted at you, rhythmically. You reach out to touch what is in front of you because you cannot believe it is happening. That there is structural space caving in, curving. That you can rotate around the same object and see all sides of it. And so it breaks apart, even the atoms. Protons, electrons, neutrons. Parts of what you thought was so whole and good. So what of it all? The answer: there are three of you, there is three of everything, the smallest bones in your body, kindly remove your clothing for closer examination, we're not quite sure how to put you back together again.

The horses and humans are living together in harmony and have been doing so for a good long while now. Nothing regarding this will change.

THE POWER IS OUT, SING

In the most senseless parts of sleep, I choose between them. Some of the nerves in my leg buzz when this happens. The act of choosing means that one is discarded. One means something far more valid. It would be easy to say: Yes, that is true, if I wasn't also, in some way, aware that I was dreaming. The act of dreaming is apparently the mind whispering secrets to you in the form of a code. All of the answers are there if you look hard enough. When I wake up, though, I can't remember who I chose in the end of the dream.

Sarah asked me to fix her bike for her, which I did. She made me put my hands on her, too, even though they were covered in grease. She didn't ask me to wash them. Her face, chest, and legs all got black. I had seen both of them like this: covered in their own mess of black. From decisions they had poorly made. And I was involved, I knew this. They shared it with me. I was covered in it, too. In ash, grease, sweat. These tattoos I never asked to have on me, this large block of metal in my stomach, these hundreds of volts of electricity inside of my house and my body.

So we had these moments of violence, him and I, it was fine. He was a boy, and I was a boy, and that was what they called us in their language. As boys our real language then was war. Sometimes this resulted in a division of skin. We fought for skin mass instead of land. I claimed most of him then: torso, small of back, hind legs, earlobes, finger prints, thighs, hips, all of what stretched the skull under hair. Parts of him were harder to understand in terms of ownership since I knew they were shared. The difference between him and her was parts of the body represented through skin as organs which were not the same organs. His organs made sense to me because they were so similar to my own. With him and I, it was apparent when one of us was unable to get through it; we were dried out. Nothing came out of us. This one thing we couldn't keep secret. Our intestines would drag on the floor. We would stare at each other, naked and embarrassed, hot in the throat, sweating, emasculated. There were no apologies or discussions—just the truth of our own body. It was worse when only one of us was able to achieve it—then the silence between us was strangling.

Sarah and I were in the dark about most things with one another. I don't mean in a way where I wasn't holding a lightbulb between my teeth or the lights were not on, because they weren't, but I don't mean that kind of dark. I never knew if she had come or not. I hardly left anything inside of her; it was habitually collected in bags and tossed, if it happened at all, and it was up to me to dispose of it. She never had a chance to examine the evidence very closely, she never asked to, never rummaged through the garbage to find it, to keep it along with the rest of her artifacts, the museum she was building. She had to figure out her own way to document it, if at all. If it was even something she wanted to remember, or could.

We stood in the dark gawking up at the moon, which was bruised with clouds crossing over it. Her face then was grains of gold and blue. My eyes were licking the light off her, hungry and having her. My stomach was still and strangely so. I did not tell her this. What was around us was just that: dark. All that was left of the Power Company Building was black and quiet.

She grabbed my hand and held it until the sweat was gone. Something was gone in her, too. She swept her hair out of her face and we wandered together around the ruins in a long silence, keeping careful not to step on possible nails or hard edges of steel. Hours passed by. And she started humming.

What are you doing, I asked her, letting go of her hand.

She smiled, huge and nauseating. She said: The power is out, sing.

I looked up at the moon and the terrible black around us and tried to hear anything else but her singing. There were crickets and cars moving in thickets thunderstorms and water rushing all in the distance and her humming was familiar to me, but I could not put my tongue right on it. I tried to block it out, the singing, and find some energy. As in: I knew there had to be additional energy sources, some small generators for blackouts, the next Power Company Building in the grid, but I could not hear it no matter how hard I shut my eyes trying to see silent films inside me, hear anything but the ordinary noise of the earth and singing from Sarah's ordinary mouth.

I opened my eyes again and looked at her squarely, as best as I could in the dark, the enormous night. I don't remember any songs, I said.

My father had a secret record collection in his closet. I figured this out by putting two and two together. As in: *math.* That song she was humming was that song he was humming, that noise that I heard in his room at night. He listened to them with what I learned to be called *headphones.* A telephone call to the skull, sing.

There were twenty-one records in the collection. Each had two songs, one on each side. I shared this with him one night. We took the box of records and my dad's record player to the treehouse. We had to unplug some of the lamps, which became an argument between us. He said that we could not unplug the lamps, what about the noise of lamps. I said that the lamps do not stop singing even when you unplug them, always is the noise of lamps. I did not invite Sarah.

In the songs, I heard what variants of colour I tasted in my dreams. Each one was different, and as we got further into the collection, the stomach ache got worse. Some of the language I used to describe this to him was: *I touch no one and no one touches me.*

The object of the record in my hands was akin to what he would call *drunk* but I would call *dizzy.* The lines carved into them were like maps leading in endless circles.

When the last record finished, he handed me a lightbulb and asked me if I was starting to feel sick again. I told him: Yes, I was. I asked him what the lightbulb was for, and he said: You will feel better. He was tender about this. Something in him seemed very different. I tried to count the colours in his eyes and they were three, again, so it was hard to tell what had changed, exactly.

I didn't ask him how he knew. I didn't bother using the language of question marks. He always seemed to be one step ahead.

I asked the doctor about sex because I wanted to know about it. I didn't use the word sex, though. I tried to ask in a very innocent way. I wanted her to believe that my body still belonged to me, that I had never once thought to share it with anyone else. Rather, I tried to word the questions hypothetically. As in: *what does it mean if*. As in: *how will I know when*. What does that have to do with what you're feeling, she asked. I tried to explain that from what I had learned in school this age for boys meant a lot of physical changes. I said: Is that why I felt sick. She said that the changes I was going through wouldn't be affecting things like my stomach, necessarily, but that it was one possible explanation. Sleep and eating patterns generally begin to change drastically around your age, she said. I wanted to ask her, *what age do you mean exactly*, but I kept my mouth shut. I asked her if there were any other boys coming into her office asking her whether or not they were swallowing fire in their sleep. She said: Doctor patient confidentiality.

The energy became completely deafening, clogging the earbones. I started to forget *information*. Once, we had ages, names, birth certificates, receipts, folders full of documentation in police offices, in hospitals. They all started to feel false. The energy turned them out, made us to forget.

We carried our illness around in jars, in pockets of our skin. They never told me directly that they had it, too. They didn't have to—I saw it in them. I saw them eating yellow at night, scraping it from each other's eyes, trying to recover the light texture in their teeth.

I woke up in the middle of the night, sweating like I thought that somehow the house was moving me closer to it. North. When he was in the bed with me, he would hold the flashlight to the sheets while we hid under them, and remind me that it was impossible for the house to move. He said: We are still.

Habitually I wore my disguise around her. The disguise being what I thought I might need to be moving closer towards her. I caught her singing in the shower. I think she was looking for something else to cure her that maybe she couldn't find in me. In the energy. In all of the houses lit up at night, between dinner hours and bedtime hours, when everyone was awake in their homes doing whatever came natural to them. Fucking, fighting, folding the laundry.

What songs she was singing I couldn't say. I asked her about some of them later, and she told me what they were called, but all of their names now are gone from me. Like *information*, except that I'd forgotten it. A small trauma to the head.

I raised my hand in class to answer a question and my arm went numb for a little while. The question was: After mitosis, are the daughter cells capable of dividing again?

I slept in the attic while I waited for my arm to heal, tossing and turning most of the night. He crawled into the window with a ladder he had stolen, to check on me. He scratched my arm as hard as he could, to try to wake it up. I only felt the pain of it days later.

The attic got wet because he left the window open accidentally and it rained. It leaked into my bedroom just below and ruined most of my books and magazines. Sarah helped me clean up the mess so my parents wouldn't find out. I woke up shaking in the night, though, thinking that my lungs were filling up with mold.

The teacher said: Yes. And then went on to explain it further with a diagram that he drew on the chalkboard. The diagram looked exactly like our treehouse somehow.

My arm healed three days before the Power Company Building was burnt down.

The police report said that the fire was arson. Sarah asked me what arson was and I explained it to her as briefly as I could: *it is when someone makes a fire on purpose.*

I asked him who he thought could've burned it down. He touched the three scars on my stomach and said he had no idea.

I took off my costume in front of him and asked him to remove his. He stared at me blankly. He broke his pause and said: I don't have a costume, what are you talking about.

Ash got caught in certain regions of my throat. This made my speech even more impossible. I did not know how to make a melody come out of me, what words would fill in the blanks of sentences, my teeth gritted. When I spoke the sounds that came out of me were foreign, unfamiliar, false.

I don't remember when or why he and I jumped off the train bridge. It was dusk at the time, it was summer, it was warm, the water was cold, it stung my body, left long red streaks on my skin for days, turning purple, I don't remember who talked who into doing it, just hitting the water with a crack that made my head feel like it was caving in, a mountain in my mouth having an avalanche, and then the plugs in the wall at night sung for me to push my head into them, to charge, to fill up with noise, to generate the lamps with my blood, to drain all of what I had of me into the wires that went all throughout the houses, and to break apart into something new again, to crack open in a splash of water. Friction. Adulthood achieved.

We made a film together of what we did, him and I, which I kept in a storage compartment in one of the walls of the attic. We would watch it together, occasionally, not touching. Not even looking at one another. Just staring at our own bodies on the screen, the unfiltered green light from the grass, the way we swallowed each other infinitely.

The film was a series of short fragments of our experiments together between the ages of ten and sixteen. I only know our ages because they are written on top of the videotape with a black marker on a white sticker, in his handwriting. He stole a video camera from his uncle and that's how we did it. He was very insistent. It was him who asked if we could watch it, too.

Sarah and I didn't have any films of the things we did. She wrote things down. Things became disjointed inside of me. I seemed to be the only one aware between all of us that a film or a journal entry or an old dress in a drawer is not necessarily a contained memory, that all of the light captured, all of that time spent hiding documents and secrets, though comforting, nostalgic, even familiar at times, was inevitably a form of fiction. The friction between our bodies, our central nervous systems, ventriloquists. Between what I thought was the end of my body, what belonged to me and could share, and his unintelligible speech, her singing the night through.

All of it became fiction, I realized. Even my own head could not contain it properly.

Once, during climax, he yelled out: You're fucking her too. And then after the silence, catching our breath, he continued: We all are. He didn't bother trying to explain this to me. My arms started to go numb under him, and I thought I would never feel it again, and I thought what a good time to lose an arm, really.

It was maybe the only thing becoming clear to me: this body doesn't belong to me, it never did, we are sharing nothing.

OF THERMAL ENERGY, THE EFFICIENT USE OF LAND AND CONTINUOUS OPERATION

+ - + - + - + - + - + - + - + A math equation I used to know was this terrible weight of the body plus the infinite weight of the rock of the earth is forests full of white wine. This textbook in my head I swallowed whole like a snake, causing nightmares, dizziness, euphoria, namelessness, running away from home on my birthday, eventual panic, locking all of the doors, unlocking all of the doors, mouthfuls of garbage, head and stomach pain, throwing up for no real reason, a sandwich my mother made in a brown bag, eventually forgetting my birthday, a ghost, a wet mattress. All of this as textbooks is coming out of me thick and wet again, like how every day I just assumed he had already forgotten my name. We had telepathic communication. I never needed to touch him, but I did, because I wanted to. I wanted to break all of the bones in his body just to have him. And then I said: a math equation I used to know was this amount of your semen in my mouth plus how much you've left inside of her is a thousand dead children, a graveyard of bedsheets, and I don't remember my own name either. On a park bench, I masturbated an old man while he talked about his sons, his daughters. He looked like he could've given birth to all of us. And in the forests, with my pants down around my ankles, running home, I felt the energy all over me. I felt it come right out of my stomach. I rewrote all of the textbooks down across my legs with a wrench, this math equation I used to know: this mother and this father is these children coming crooked from the bunkers, false fire crackers in their mouths, my house is on fire I told you this before. My head is on fire, and I've got the dictionary in my mouth, but I can't swallow it. A dictionary is just another book filled with words. A curse word jar. If I ate enough of the language I thought I would be able to heave my own ambiguity. How terrified I was. Am. And fix? Fix being alarm clocks, telephones, computers. This is *fix*. This is all being digested by me. How much could my body handle: it's basic. A humidifier. An entire soundtrack of cars. All of the energy from all of the houses. How can they all enjoy their dinner, so much with their mouths, I wondered, when I'm eating it all for them. When there's fire in everything we eat. He said we're swallowing fire in our sleep. I woke with my tongue burnt, my limbs being pulled apart by an entire league of doctors and professional technicians. Linguists who feared I was eating their language. Everything they had studied so hard. In the x-rays of my stomach, they also found lava lamps, stethoscopes, plastic bags, dishwashers, strawberry banana pancakes. They said I would run out of room, but I knew I would never be full. I took all of what I could. I came apart at the seams. My ears were filled with many train parts. I had a hundred men, all lined up, ready for me to let them do what their wives wouldn't. They passed through me. They told me they could tell when I hadn't brushed my teeth. When my mouth tasted like other men. When it had been a busy night in general. For everyone, for all of us, the streets covered in bed comforters, pulled off, and television sets no one wanted anymore, we were all going blind a little bit, what was the point.

Which will tear what object when. He has canopies over his eyelids and he is buttering his skin, all ways of avoiding the subject. He is all categories and articles of clothing we keep trading, back and forth, as if they don't belong to anyone. Ownership being just one part of the long indoctrination process, and how eventually we would come to, clean, and remember we have nothing. What I want to ask him is: can he set up categories for my wild, make room for it in his drawers, pull back up his pants when he is finished filling me up? I wait and wait for his wild, for him wild and fucking me to fill me. What rather would I be than a pocket and a place to keep some of him. Is he not static. Yes. Is he material moving everywhere. Yes. And can he find me, my wild. The three of us all move in circular motion, I watch him through windows fucking her up against the bed, like two elephants that haven't eaten in months. A prayer is all these suitcases packed and me pillaging through the graveyard for a million things to say. Looking for anybody who would be willing to share fluid instead of dialogue, conversation. Like: I am staring at The Canon, right? But it has no eyes? Like: I am waiting for five hundred books to fill up my stomach, but all I am is heavy with fire and flood. And all the names here are slowly leaving my head. All the songs, too.

We roast, together, in the company of the burning sun. I am accustomed to this. I am prepared for the scorching of the violins that hold me together. Each of us thinking: what about water, look at our skin and how it cooks, a good dinner we are trembling too hard to eat. Perfectly, each time, this happens. By night, when the heat is heavier on the houses, when it collapses around the gardening sheds, we stay outside for hours at a time, lingering around the radio towers. This transmission I received that night was: *All duty is dream all you are is wildfires.* And I wake up and my mouth is black bear fur instead of fine bone and tissue and I cannot get him or it out of me. I followed the two of them and watched how they could accept each other briefly and then part ways. Before I would go to meet him, I would track her to see what kind of afterglow she had. And she was sick with it. She looked delirious, like she would never fuck again, as if the idea of it was enough to tire her out entirely. She never looked that way when we were done, her eyes gunshot with powder, the two of us parading in and out of the cemeteries until the sun came back up and we cooked again, ready to be eaten by dinner time.

A reminder of all the good green light: you having the rest of your body taken away as parts of a system (that works, re-acts, stays central, godless, is in the same room as both you and what made you). I taught thieves how to take their clothes off. The art of good bedroom posing. What I want is for you to understand that this body is not my body, it is theirs. We are all in it: three broken pieces that can never be put back together. This is not about halves and wholes. Although they did find holes in me. Old and new. The ends of my hands coming off. I could not explain this to them. I had to watch all three of us stay in the same pattern, knowing parts of me belonged to them, were growing from my own rejuvenated skin. Sharing it as opposed to healing, stretching it out into canvas, into leather. I am too tired to try to pull what you need of me out. It is buried in dead nerves on my arms from handcuffs that will not heal. It is being held down to the ground and told to be a good dog, a good fuck, a good friend. And I am anything but these things. For example: the fact that we are all bored to death is obvious. I have spent enough time in emergency rooms to know that even when everyone is in extreme panic, all alarmed, at the center of all this anxiety there is boredom. I am not going to attempt to articulate where this boredom comes from. But I have had men inside me without antlers, who are all hard in the right places and everything, but who have nothing to say before, during, or afterwards. They have fumbled around enough to know how to get through it. And we do. We fuck our way through it. We singe our sore parts and pass them around as if they have never belonged to us or anybody. And we blame all of the quiet on the energy, on the fact that no one will understand us if we do talk. I have been with plaid-covered men, collapsed on beer-bellies sleeping in the woods after a fuck (disjointed, surrounded by heavy wood, eating mushrooms to stay alive). I have had beards tough against my face, antlers dug into my back, scraping the blood into their mouths, and bucking their hips heavy and hard, saying how sweet it is to have more of me than anyone, my knees skinning against the bark of trees, tangled in the heads of husbands.

Piano variations I got in me while we were sharing ourselves. While I had some left of myself to share. Piano parts all re-arranged in my head until they were music too. A lot of what was me was kindling. A bag on my head, walking down the street, filling all jars of me with meat, and all jars of me with the meat of the horses, and all jars of me with the meat of the horses' hands. I walk from one side of the room to the other hoping that the other side of the room will have less metal in the oxygen, but I continue breathing it. Swiftly I do this. She unties the knots that I've started growing in between my legs from all this nightrunning. I ask her to dig me out of this because I want to know which of us came first. How do we celebrate our birthdays when we don't know them. We stopped having birthdays. No more blown out candles. I don't know my birthday and I have forgotten my own name. During introductions now, I am quiet, we shake just hands. And I can see it in their faces: they don't remember, either. There is no point anymore in knowing these things about ourselves. What is important now is what order to put ourselves back together in. I decided it was me who had to go first. All of that static in my head, those narcissistic knives splitting through me. I got what I wanted, right. The entire population density to be just that. Dense. Thick and swarming. Good god I wanted it. It was beautiful. Standing there without my body anymore. I buckled over, legs spread open farther than they can go, pulling away from me, in all directions. He says: We should get dressed. As if that was even a possibility. Standing there without my clothes on, without my body, I pushed him off of me, hard, threw him into the wall, splintering the wood, and I pushed him down and stuck myself inside of him, inside of her, inside of us, inside of the great white walls of Heaven we all contained but could not see in our blindness. And he let me have at him like a dog, scraping his skin off as I fucked him roughly, and I forgot his name again, mine, the mailman. I pulled out so fast that what I thought I would leave inside of him all came spilling out, all over the bedroom floor, and he looked at me with bruises on his eyes, like: how could you do this, how could you do this to me, what do you want. I said: We can't pretend we are clean anymore, when's your birthday? And he stared back at me, his eyes filled heavy with water and rust, and said: I don't remember. My tactics were animals in me now. Fuck and forget we ever felt sick, eat all of the electricity in the house as midnight snacks, they have won.

He told me he was sick and I didn't really want to listen to him. He was indecisive. He used so little language. Words like *yes* and *no* and *now* and *not now*. He left doors open all of the time. I told him I was scared shitless. Of what was happening to the three of us. Her, running around in her mother's dresses, and him, always having to leave the room to throw up again. Asking me to put the maps away, he didn't want to see them. Plugging his ears in geography class. I thought, while he was in me, that maybe he was transferring it to me. The sickness, that is. Somehow giving me a little bit of it, only tiny pieces at a time. And I would walk around afterwards, all of him sloshing inside me, suddenly knowing how all the tigers could see green in the ocean. How we're all walking on the smaller parts of the sun. Feeling the ends of me as God knows what. Like he could've pollinated me, we could've made more of each other, more sick kids running through hospitals. I followed them into the woods, to watch them. This was habit. I have video evidence of this: the fact that our bodies had all been shared. I had a secret box of tapes that neither of them knew about. They made promises to one another. Mostly: him to her. Mostly: *I will love you forever.* Dangerous four-letter words. These words they never used with me. She said: Fuck me. He said: Fuck you. She looked like she was hungover, full too much with blood. I had to wonder if she ever followed us, to find out what he was doing to me. I definitely wasn't telling her, and neither was he. We called this *secrets*. The same as me sneaking her his father's record collection, one at a time. The same as me running with snot coming down my face, and yes, scared shitless, that they would find out, that all of the horses would eventually eat me, that we were running out of time before it happened of its own accord. I wanted to save them from it. I wanted all of us to wake up one morning, clean and painless, and I thought: why wait, I can end this all, I've been starting a fire my entire life, why stop now.

I think we would all have agreed we spent most nights trembling from too many unanswered questions, and that our beds needed to be burned if to make them clean. The reality of how much we had been in them—our beds, that is—over periods of time, with one another, or how much we made our beds out of other locations—was enough to make us want to rub our heads against a washboard until it was gray with blood. I said to her: You hit me close to home like a rock to the temple, I am dizzy now with dreams. And it was true. Our resources were running out. Our questions were not being answered by anyone physically, anyone verbally. I heard what I thought maybe were answers shifting through various rooms in the house, but the words they spoke were inaudible. I had a bag on my head and I was breathing only myself back in. She was sucking most of the earth through a milkshake straw from the corner store, biased because of the berries she had eaten from me earlier, bored because of no other available flavours. Just him and I both tasting the ends of lightbulbs. Like electroshock therapy on the human tongue, dried and held out with prongs, a hundred hands trying to pull it from the mouth. I achieved my own spine coming split out of me, vertebrae once vertical now aligned with the hands of horizons. All attempts at retaining my bones in me were failures. I could try again another time. The lack of sleep in my lungs earning me a new medallion: courage, recklessness, pride. My headaches were from too much sunlight at one time. I wanted only that light which was artificial. My eyes were profiting from the slow relax and deduction of my vision, the time it takes to go blind, the blotches of blue when blinking now permanent, colourless, odourless. See: it was me who showed her the energy, despite what she might say. Before either of us even really knew what to make of it. We were ten, taut and tickling, running around in the evenings, starting to stay up later than we should. I found the energy and I showed it to her, and she showed it to him. My headaches were eased only by lamplight and lingering in the treehouse for long periods of time in the general blackness that was the forest. The only light being that which was created from us and from the Power Company Building. From the energy that we were producing with it. It wasn't long after I taught her about it that we started to explore each other's bodies, and his; together, separately.

Dancing in parking-lots, drunk, listless, screaming, blowing old men, arcades and malls everywhere instead of fire, books I stole from the library, books I put in my head for safe keeping. He gave me a photograph of his mother to carry in my wallet instead of a photograph of him. He said: This is where I came from and that's what more important and this is my real face. I wanted to tell him that he doesn't even know her, but instead more liquid in my lungs, on my face, bathroom stalls in the winter, a good hundred graves grown around me while I am sleeping on this photograph, losing pinball, a sense of where I put my cutlery, where to put laundry in my mouth, roam, roam, roar. It was like this for a long time. I was so good when I had them in me. I didn't feel like I was being tamed or put into cupboards, closets, secret parts of attics. This is where I knew most people put what they didn't want: clothes, sons and daughters. I wondered: why have them. Sons or daughters, these people who just had to share their fluid with someone else, just so they could create something that later they would be ashamed of. A choir in my head was singing me this. They said I was running out of water. There were instructions as to how to solve this problem, none of which involved drinking anything. They were: *Put a mattress between you and the wall and stay there, sleep there, standing up, it's the only way.* And I stood there like they told me to until I felt nothing hanging between my legs anymore. Nothing weighing me down. As if it was removed from me by secret surgeons, quietly. An exorcism of the sex I once had. The cleanest sheets I owned pressed against my skin. All until I erupted again, in my sleep, covering the mattress with it, leaking all over the house for days as I walked around, back out the door, into the woods, looking for something new to fill me back up. When very late nights fill the room, I attempt to insert language, but I only have hands and my shoes untied on the floor and all of it only mine temporarily. He says to me that he is obsessed with this idea, of us not talking. I am alright with the quiet. I would like more silence and less worrying and more noise in my head that is like the noise that I hear when I am very near to a window, leaning my head out and wondering when the earth will lift me away. I used to write sentences that spilled, very quickly it all came out of me; now it's all out slow, over periods of time. I want to talk about meat and bedspreads and the tattoos I will never have and what he looks like, right there, in that lighting. Mosquito bites, too. How they are all hungry, as hungry as we all are, and how we're all feeding from the same essential source. The sun on my face. The marrow of leaves. The lawyers lending their time to juveniles. Cutting all of our hair to be the same. How this is just it: meat, bedspreads, tattoos, mosquito bites. Being tickled to death in your sleep. Finding my rollerblades, which somehow were removed from my feet while still in motion, later at the bottom of the lake, home to thousands of fish chewing. I heard him when he asked me: How come we have everything? But I didn't answer because I figured it was obvious. We are eating it. This entire landscape of filth. We have everything because it's what we asked for, it's what we wanted, and it wasn't enough. It wasn't enough so I had to have more. For three days, I hid from the cops. I was confused, yes, I thought that all parts of me were transmitting radio frequencies and they could track me down. But then I remembered that all of the evidence against me was burned, and there was no proof, and that no one would even really think to suspect me, except perhaps Sarah, who would never go to the police with information anyways. She knew too much of it herself, she slept with dead horses, in the clawed linen of dried semen. So I didn't have to keep hiding. In fact, I might as well have just yelled it out in the streets: I did it, it was me, you fuckers, it was all of us, we did this together, your body doesn't end where you think it does, so will you talk now, let's talk now. See: we were all quiet, but it was dishonest. We really did have a lot to say.

The difference between the three of us is only physical location. And see us all moving here. The location is impermanent. It is temporary. I sweat nights through thinking about where they were and how I could find them when they were moving and I, too, was moving, scathing across the lawns of local townspeople, letting myself loose on the forest. I had a bad dream once about a card game that went all wrong, and I went blind, and I started a fire. I did it on purpose because I had to make an answer somehow in what categories of answers were available to me. A sickness that courses through you can cause certain amounts of physical distress, yes, but it can also close off your options, and your head starts to spin with what options are left. She said: Water. I said: Fire. He said: Energy. We all threw up horsehair in the night. The mattresses left in the woods were all full of our various fluids. Of strangers. I was vapour to him while he slipped himself in and out of me. She was vapour to me while I slipped myself in and out of her. It made sense to wrangle up strangers with us since we were all estranged from one another in our own way. Our bodies were changing, too—independently, at their own speeds, completely out of our control. I did not want to be safe. I wanted to share the body that I had as it was with nothing between us. And the textbook said that two things never touch directly, not really, because there are moving particles between the particles that make us up, and so there is always a distance, even if minute. I wanted nothing of the distance. I wanted to get rid of it. I didn't care about being clean; I was fine with having sores on me, with the pains of growing. I wondered: what about three, can three things ever touch, if two can't, do we meet in a triangular room somewhere, creating, somehow, a solid that cannot be broken. Does the language that we share save us from this distance at all, can we form some sort of wall. I got the blood from my head in the river and on their beds. I left trails of it through the woods, trying to find them, pressing my mouth against their foreheads. I wobbled in and out of states, the pitch of the radio transmissions whining and piercing more holes in the heads of deer, of dandelions, of dogs. Of me and the matter that made me, the mother that I never had who somehow had me, and a group of boys wandering through the woods with me all wearing red and yellow, delirious as if they had not struck any amount of food in months, all the while holding the blood from my head on my hands and asking the hands why they did not come off of me, rolling around in their bedsheets, singing no songs at all, catching the jaws of my skull on their collarbones, and hanging off the top of the bunk bed, knocking all of the teeth from me, all of the seed from me, sewn into their clothes again with dried semen, all that's left of me, choirs the whole time holding me down and telling me, it's time.

SYNESTHESIA

NOW THEN

Three children is always worse than one. One child can, and does, cause damage, but in this instance, and only in this instance, one child only causes damage because of three children. A broken mouth seed. A policeman or a fireman would have a lot to say about the minds of children if they knew the minds of children. A policeman or a fireman could be you if you were standing in front of a physical crime or fire. Would you be able to tell the difference between the children who caused damage because they have been left alone long enough and those who were waiting impatiently for you to leave the room, with damage in mind the entire time? The reasons for committing a crime, though discussed at length, are usually not even known to the criminal themselves, and especially in the case of children. If three children make water, fire, and energy, then which child brings forth the food for eating, the hours for sleeping? As in: three children sing with their mouths closed, which is not to say that they hum, and they carry around a sickness which is the same sickness, which is a different sickness, which is all of the closets open, revealing the skeletons. One fire is enough to take away power for one week. Three fires are not necessary. Three children are necessary for one fire, even if only one child uses their actual physical hands to make it, even if only one child has the guts to ask the question, the arm raised for so long it goes numb.

THE "IT" DISEASE

A common cold is similar to the disease of being It. In the case of a common cold, the disease is spread through germs, through close contact. In the case of It, It is spread through language. If language is a potential disease, some might wonder why anyone would speak at all. A Blue who is colour blind may wonder why they are called a Blue, but may lack the language to ask such a question. A Purple is a Purple because Purple has been decided on as a colour. A family is a family because it has been decided on by blood. Some who might wonder who is It in the first place might never find an answer to their question. Two teams think that they are It: Greens and Blues. What would it mean then, if a Green were to confront a Blue and spread this disease through language? Can you catch an illness that you already have?

THE POWER COMPANY BUILDING

The Power Company Building is noiseless and broken down into its smallest parts. The actual physical weight of the remaining ash is still a denomination of three and is also still prime, and the pond nearby is now mostly plants attempting to regain strength and ducks in serious shock all from seeing fire, a blinding amount of red heat that scorched the treetops, spread to graves, met the pond and stood at the shore of it pounding and bellowing, the fences all turned into skeletons, bones broken into three, a fire at three, involving three, seen from three kilometers, three dead ducks actually, three sleeping neighbours woken up to blindness, three deaths that year already, three dogs who were brothers, who were sisters, who were sick and couldn't walk, and yes, one of them had three legs. The smallest parts of you are the ears that allow you to hear the noise of fire. Remember?

AFTER

Kinesthesia leaves the Power Company Building and goes back into the woods, leaving pieces of his clothes in his path. All of the evidence that could be traced toward him is only the clothing from his body, which is collected up by a member of the Orange team later in the night. Thermal Energy follows him, keeping a close eye, as close as one can in the pitch black of some forests. The woods are filled with men and children and trees. The difference between men and children and trees is how they move around in the woods. A tree is a stable thing which does not appear to move side to side or in any direction except up or down, and this it does slowly. Some of the trees are waiting to grow to Heaven, which is impossible. Kinesthesia could easily be confused for a man but is a child, climbing up trees. Some other children are using trees as hiding places or spots to take brief naps. Kinesthesia's fever begins to fade, which only causes him to want to share it more and more. He waits up in the branches and watches the men wander around below him, wondering who to share it with before it is gone from him entirely. Thermal Energy puts his hands on Kinesthesia's forehead to check his temperature and feels the decline. The Efficient Use Of Land has stopped singing, content now to be fat and sleeping, getting his skin cooked good by fire. Synesthesia is on the outside of the True North side of the woods by the highway, not noticing any of this, except for the sound of police sirens in the distance, which he ignores. He has, by this hour, counted twenty-seven cars pass by. He has been keeping count with a marker on his wrist in tally format, grouped into fives. There are five finished tallies and one unfinished tally with two. The cars seem to come only in groups of two, three, or six, in a span of several minutes. The glow of a diner sign is opposite him on the highway, and there are several trucks parked outside. When no cars are going by, he counts men in the diner. This he keeps track of on his opposite wrist, though this list does not go up as frequently because of the late hour. He feels a strange tingling in his stomach that is different than the usual feeling he has in that particular portion of his body, but does not think much of it at this point. Sarah sits patiently in the stables, trying to keep her eyes open, focusing on the horse next to her. She hears the sirens, too, but they are farther away from her, and she is far too focused on the horse to care or worry. She does, however, leave several times to throw up in one of the troughs. Other Alterations holds back her hair. Moving Water has been leaving the horses: it has bigger fish to fry. It has fire to fight. To fight fire is to *extinguish* or *put out*. The fire is spreading from the Power Company Building to surrounding trees and the firefighters do just that, fight fire, arms out, hoses out, bundled up in smoke.

MOVING WATER

There is no Moving Water in certain horses. Yes, horses have blood, horses drink water, horses beat the ground into mud, which is water and dirt, which is sweat and salt and earth. But Moving Water can choose when to leave. It can ask young girls to drain horses. It can even be fed, over and over again, into the mouth of someone who is thirsty and not even for a moment quench the thirst. This is how Mister Lonely dies. This is how young girls are responsible for the deaths of horses. When was the last time you asked your water what it wanted?

AFTER

Synesthesia falls asleep on the side of the highway for many hours and does not wake up. The unfinished tally list on his arm reached forty-two cars, twelve men. One of the men he has previously counted leaves the diner after he has finished his coffee and toast, and instead of going back to his truck, he walks off in the direction of South, into the woods. The leader of the Blue team emerges from almost the same spot, and they pass one another quietly. Quietly but not without speaking. The Blue saying: *Sir*. The man saying: *Blue*. The leader of the Blue team sees Synesthesia's sleeping body in the brush on the shoulder of the highway, and pokes at him with a stick. Synesthesia does not respond to the poking, so the leader of the Blue team assumes him dead and rolls his body down away from the highway further into a ditch. The man walks about a mile into the woods, at which point he sees Kinesthesia up in a tree, and targets him by pulling on his ear, like a signal. Kinesthesia, recognizing the signal clearly, climbs down the tree to join the man, and they both walk together to the collection of mattresses, between three trees. This being the location on the earth where Synesthesia and Kinesthesia had been together not even twenty-four hours earlier. The man pulls down his pants just enough and takes off his shirt, unfastening each button carefully, watching as Kinesthesia removes the entirety of his clothing from his body. They pile their clothes together in the dirt, both smelling of gasoline, of smoke. Some men and some children smell of gasoline, of smoke. The lightning in the sky is false; some children only dream it. There is smoke in the sky. There is Moving Water moving through pipes and hoses, through the heads of mothers who have dreamt of fire, who have drowned themselves. Several other men and children are dispersed throughout a six mile radius in the woods doing only the kinds of things that men and children do together in the dark, in the night. True North watches children and men in the dark all at once with what is known as *omnipotence*. One member of the Orange team has forfeited the game, having joined a man on one of the mattresses, having stolen Kinesthesia's clothes. Some children sing of fire, some men of water, and the swimmers stay swimming and the fires keep burning, and sleepers stand awake in the street watching the only light left.

EROSION

Heavy rain loosens the soil. Heavy fire causes the rock of the earth to crack. Rainstorms have been coming back and forth from the same central source, from here to there, only as a deliberate attempt to break apart certain masses of land. Fires have been made on purpose to crack the soil. Erosion is the ecosystem being changed slowly during mostly nighttime hours such as this. Erosion takes direct command from True North and listens closely for orders. When True North is silent, there are draughts, there are no fires, there is in fact no movement in the earth at all.

AFTER

When Sarah returns to the stable, the horse is already dead.

OTHER ALTERATIONS

Other Alterations makes all of her socks into sock puppets and performs a one-act play about the burning down of the Power Company Building exactly in time with the actual event, word-for-word.

Other Alterations cuts off the ends of her socks and makes them into shoulder pads for certain blouses, certain dresses that have not yet been worn or wanted.

Other Alterations does an interpretative dance concerning the death of Mister Lonely, which includes the use of her bedsheets as elegant gowns and a full score of funeral marches.

Other Alterations eats all of the jewelry in her room because Other Alterations has a hankering for gold and silver.

Other Alterations does get lonely, yes, keep her company.

THE "IT" DISEASE

There is no time for sleep during a game like this, but some boys feel the need to break some rules, which include cat naps in trees, bushes, sand dunes, park benches, which include being with some men on some mattresses. Green is It and Blue is It, which inevitably makes no one It and cancels out the game. This has not yet been made known to anyone, since no one from any team has seen any other member of their team for most of the night. A game that is *over* could be referred to as *work*, but in this instance, there is no language for it. The game that is *over* continues as if only by necessity, default.

THERMAL ENERGY

The problem with having a plan all along is how hard it is to keep it a secret. If you are attempting to coerce someone into doing something that they might not want to do, this is one thing. But when the one you're trying to coerce really only needs that little shove, that last little bit to push them over the edge and do what they've been wanting to do all this time, it's absolutely titillating. There are many ways to ensure someone will do what you want them to. One of these ways is to repeat the command over and over again, until the request becomes ingrained. This can be done with words as well as with images. This can be done with dreams. The problem here, then, is *blame*. Who is to *blame* for a fire that was started by one person, but delicately planned by everyone, all at once? Yes, you are complicit. You can stop moving in your seat now. Yes, that is an order.

NOW THEN?

The fire is out after several hours of fighting it. A fire can only burn for so long when there are fire hunters looking to stop it dead. When Moving Water has killed horses for fire. This night, then, is mostly silent. This night is a pitch-black night since there is no artificial light to help guide the eyes from one place to another. Some would have taken more kindly to blindness if they closed their eyes once in a while and thought about what they'd done. Even the insomniac mothers are sleeping, standing up in the middle of the kitchen. There is nothing left to see without energy. No good dull sound of appliances, no man-made white noise to lull you comfortably in your bed or sofa. Without energy, certain sicknesses even seem to stop for a moment.

AFTER

Kinesthesia leaves the woods by taking a trail he has memorized so well with his body that his blindness in the dark does not deter him. He walks, splayfooted, naked, with his arms out in front of him to feel the way with the arm portions of his body, scarring them on broken branches which jut out intermittently along the path. He wanders through the streets, staring into the dark windows of buildings, admiring signs no longer lit up. The heavy sound of no clocks ticking, no power lines buzzing. Only sirens singing. He ducks briefly behind a bush as a fire truck goes by, the sound suddenly deafening. He keeps low, walking behind houses and through yards to get back to his own house, where he crawls in through the window and goes to sleep. True North laughs heartily through the night, but the sound is not heard by anyone except for his brother, who has spent the greater part of the night trying to figure out the logistics of the fire itself: with what made, with what put out. Sarah does not sleep. She stays with Mister Lonely until he dies, at which point she smells smoke. Other Alterations takes all of the bones out of the horse's body and grinds them into sand. Sarah leaves the stables as the light begins to strike the sky again, having had heavy eyes for hours. She walks, barefoot, from the racetrack, into town, past the woods (not entering them), and down to the docks, where she sits, smoking cigarettes. Sarah knows what has happened because of the temperature of the water, the lack of texture in the noise of the earth, the smoke half-hazard in the sky. Synesthesia's body stays still in a ditch. Kinesthesia's body, relieved of fever, stays still in bed. His head has stopped singing; there is no choir banging and swelling in him now. All of these bodies have been shared. Sarah knows this. Other Alterations fills one of the boxes from her room with the ground bones of the dead horse and carries it to the dock. Sarah and Other Alterations perform a ritual, releasing the minced marrow as if ashes, while Sarah sings what is called a *song*. This is not considered to be a funeral. Horses don't have funerals.

THE EFFICIENT USE OF LAND

You would think with a name like that, any fat singer would know what they were singing. But then there are untilled farms, urban wastelands, ghost towns, odd machines, old factory buildings, swamps converted into highways. The Efficient Use Of Land would like to stop all of this, but sometimes the mouth is too full up with food to speak out, and the singing takes too long, the teeth hurt for too many hours afterwards.

AFTER

Synesthesia wakes up and becomes _____ . Without his illness, this false name can no longer be used for him. Without the energy, there is no illness. There is no searching for North in the night without wonder, worrying about brothers that cannot be found. Those who are nameless now remain nameless. True North has taken a compass from the human stomach and put it into his diary, for safekeeping. _____ rolls over in the ditch, collecting the water around him. Other Alterations has carved his real name onto the bottoms of his feet, but he cannot read the language of them. He gets up, brushes himself off and looks down at his arms. All of the tally marks he had written before sleep are gone. This doesn't concern him for the moment. He feels at his stomach only to notice there is no pain, other than the slight tinge of hunger. He looks around in the ditch to try to find the metal that was in his stomach, coughed up, but comes up with nothing. He walks, wayward, almost as if drunk, across the street, and up to the diner, which he realizes is closed. There are no trucks in the parking lot. All of the lights are off. The sun stings his eyes. He turns around and follows the highway to the exit that takes him down the road, which leads to the pond next to the Power Company Building. The water is still without ducks. He gets close enough only to see several police cars and a gathering crowd being pushed back by policemen. Mister Lonely stands in the middle of the ash, unseen.

CONTINUOUS OPERATION

For example: the fire killed Continuous Operation. In fact: Continuous Operation was a part of the plan from the beginning. It was a set-up. He had no say in this. His ghost, i.e. the remains of his physical body and the spirit that was contained within it released onto the earth for unfinished business (i.e. poker, revenge), is now called Stillness. Revenge is obtained by waving the arms of the body up and down frantically in a public space, such as the local dollar mart and/or a local nightclub spot. Poker is played using the dream portion of the headspace, which also includes the revealing of secrets sometimes spoken. Stillness stands in the ruins, plotting revenge. A horse is with him.

AFTER

Sarah and _____ meet later on in the day, once they have each had a proper amount of good, clean sleep. This sleep being done because the body is entirely free of that which has kept them awake for so long, clawing at the walls of bedrooms, of attics. This being done in makeshifts beds without birthing, with linens and lying down. They meet in secret because both of their parents have restricted them to the house for fear of certain vandals that could be out there. School is also cancelled. They meet at the hub of mattresses in the woods, next to the three big trees. Sarah sits, unknowingly, on the mattress that _____and Kinesthesia had fucked on the day before. _____ stands. Stillness stands between both of them, quietly. Neither of them bothers with accusations about the cause of the fire, and neither of them acknowledges the lack of sickness. Instead, they talk about horses. Were you there when he died, _____ asks her. No, I was puking, she says. Moving Water runs rivers red and roars. Kinesthesia pisses himself in his sleep, but does not wake up, nestled now in his own urine, the dreamscape of his head quiet. _____ puts his hands out to her and touches her hair. It's not your fault, he tries to assure her. She glares up at him, violently for just a moment, but quickly puts a mask over this. As in *to hide the real face*. Maybe, let's go there tonight to see it, Sarah suggests. _____ pauses for a long time before saying: There is nothing to see. Having been there himself already. Knowing that what is there now is vacancy, ash, blackness. He takes his hands off her head and lingers for a moment, before sitting down on another mattress a few feet away from her. Unknowingly, he is sitting on the mattress that Kinesthesia and the man from the diner had fucked on the night before. I'm curious, she insists. He looks her in the eye. She gets up and sits down next to him, putting her hands just underneath his t-shirt, feeling along the sides of him for something. They fuck and forget for a while. No one witnesses this interaction, not even them. They keep their eyes closed the whole time. This is also the first and only time that they fuck without protection, without a distance between them in the form of latex. He leaves some of himself inside of her. They dress slowly afterwards, collecting their clothes from the ground, plucking them up from the terrain where they have been left and laid. They are silent for a long time. *The ordinary noise of the earth.* The Efficient Use Of Land with his hands over his mouth, muting. Erosion beneath them, tearing at the bodies of worms. He looks her over, follows the long lines of thread in her dresses, the weight of her eyes on him pricking the skin's edge. Hey, he says, grabbing her shoulder like he is in some kind of a panic suddenly. What is my name, he asks. She looks at him like she doesn't recognize him at all, scanning her brain for a while like she knows there must be a name for him that exists somewhere. Finally, she says: You're Sarah, aren't you?

NORTH

Three bones broken into three pieces each and then delivered to various geographic locations (one for each direction except north, to which nothing is delivered except electricity and ash). All of the bones originated from the arms and shoulders. South gets the Humerus, west the Bursa, east the Acromion. South identifies the Humerus as mostly illiterate bone tissue escaping the wide open blowholes of whales. The Humerus, unable to justify its own case at the time, unable to speak at all really, accepts this analysis with open arms, jumping back into the open ocean. West is all about harbouring the Bursa and making it a part of the immediate family. Another brother to get the table ready for the time of eating. The Bursa, an orphan, finally with a home, settles into his role well. East has a tribunal to decide whether or not Acromion has any diseases that could be transmitted through various forms of contact (open mouth kissing, penetration, sharing the same bathroom). The tests are inconclusive and kept classified by the government, and the Acromion is released back into the wild to fend for itself. After bed, all three bones sing euphorically the same song in sleep— they wake up with pieces of themselves rejuvenated. Like they could grow the whole body back at any time but they prefer it slow. Like what is the point in growing the body back when it just means movement, responsibility. This is how parts of policemen

are made into police, how parts of children become adults, parts
of you me, of water fire.

THE "IT" DISEASE

In the late morning, the Oranges, Blues, Purples, and Greens all meet up on the beach. One of the Purples is still missing a shirt; the Blue leader lost it during the night. This boy now considers himself the sole member of the Skin team. He says: I am the Skin team. For a while, there is an argument about who is It, but they realize that this argument is futile. By noon, they are all free of disease, running back into their houses only to find no televisions to watch, no radios to sing along to. The Reds and Yellows are never seen or heard from again.

TRUE NORTH

Your logic is useless. You rely too much on what I will refer to as *trust*. What is *truth* when all information is in flux? When the earth itself is moving? If one plus one plus one equals three on one day, does it not mean that on another it will equal fire? These numbers in your head, these math equations that you used to know, are just like the body, the earth: *growing*. Do you really believe in just XX or XY, Girl or Boy? What about North and True North? These are all just words to describe direction, organs. She has This and he has That. She has an Egg and he has a Sperm. Language does exist for the purpose of distinguishing between one and another. But in the middle of the night, the mattresses are being flipped over. The magnetic energy of the earth is shifting. One day, North will be South. And then who are you going to *trust*? Which language will you rely on to get you where you want to go, to point out the difference between This and That?

NOW THEN

The things that happen in the dark—and this kind of dark, especially—are generally quiet for long periods of time, interrupted or separated into parts or halves or thirds by staccato shouts and outbursts. As in: long relaxing periods of slow Moving Water period, and then a few commas inserted of rapid movement, all close together but identified by the smaller silences in between. These silences (the small ones) consist of holding one's breath between blows, going underwater briefly, shock, terror, the alarming realization that even in the dark without sight you do indeed have a physical body which can be (and is being) experienced by oneself and others even without the light. The loud parts are interventions, family fights, early onsets of paranoia, orgasms (shared or alone), and other primal releases which contain sound both whole and sanctuary. In the silence of a blackout, parts of your body that you forgot were there entirely will start to ring out, deafeningly, and you will hear it and wonder who else is hearing it, too. The small of your back, the nail clippings you left on kitchen floors, the rough parts of your feet and kneecaps. There is a difference that should be understood between energy (as in that which you can feel all around you in a metaphysical sense or as in that which will turn the lights on in your house) and the light itself. It should be understood that a conductor such as the Power Company Building only emits *one kind* of energy. Energy, otherwise, is highly multiple. This is how you experience your body and the bodies of others even in the dark and even without contact. In the case of Synesthesia, however, the *only* energy he could feel was that which was produced by the Power Company Building itself. In the dark, he could only eventually make out faint smells as circular, touching the wood floors and carpets when he was hungry. Finally, now, just through contact, he could understand the carpentry that went into his house, the foundation and the paint fumes and the structure all being held together by precise angles. A blackout in a person is similar to that of a town; everything that happens during such an episode, whether it be brief or lengthy and large in duration, is vague and seems like a good dream, the kind that you wake from wet and wasted, as though you didn't even sleep at all. Most people who experience a blackout in their body are not even aware that anything has happened to them. They don't wonder why they are in their neighbour's yard, or the ditches of dirt roads. Setting a fire to their own house. Or to a Power Company Building. Do you understand the implications of this fact? You cannot trust your own body. It is lying to you. A power out, being in all of that black, will remind you that there are entire parts of you that you are not aware of at all, that you are forcing yourself to forget. All your actions which you thought were under your rational and logical control are in fact animalistic, instinctual, and cannot be contained by what you would call *decisions*. Imagine all of the things that you could be doing. You probably burned it down yourself and you don't even know it. All of that freedom got you good in the throat. And it is terrifying, yes, that there seems to be no explanation for all of these things that happen, but it's no good being scared of sleeping just because of what you may be doing in dreams.

THE POWER IS OUT, SING

He was losing himself in the woods more. By the time I found him, he was bleeding all over the place, hungover with sweat, swollen struck up and down on his back. He said: All the scars I have on me are from dogs. I couldn't get inside him, he was blistered, he had locked his head closed. He barely spoke. I almost had to start talking to fill in the long silences. I had no idea what language to use around him. He held onto my stomach and rubbed the blood from his hands onto me. Into my navel. All of the violence in him had gone quiet, severely. He now accepted it wholeheartedly in a way that I think he believed to be brave. In a way where he let them do whatever they needed to do to him, whatever they wanted, and he did not protest. He would have let me do anything that I wanted to. He would have let me hold him down in the bathtub and drown him, if that was what I wanted. And I had to ask because it was eating away at me, gnawing on the better parts of my organs, if I was just another dog to him. If he considered the marks I left on him to be the same as the marks that they did.

She folded the bedsheets the same as always, all of her laundry in clean piles around the room. Her terrible mouth singing. I silently moved clothes from the piles into drawers. She said: The human and the machine mouth singing simultaneously.

His last moment of violence with me that I could recall was about one week after the power came back on. He entered me forcefully, for the first and only time, without asking, holding me down to the ground, asking me if I remembered what our birthday was, if I knew who I was, or he was, or she was, at all. And I realized that I didn't know the answer to any of those questions, so I let him finish. I let him fill me.

I slept the night through better than I ever had, all the while dreaming of the songs I would sing if I was a singer, and the noise I would make if I was electricity, and how really, I didn't make any sound at all.

Our birthday party guests were all lying on the floor, on their backs, sprawled out and sleeping. She was hanging glow stars from the ceiling with fishing line and scotch tape. He was in the kitchen heating up cake batter in the oven, cracked eggs and flour all over his hands. I was wondering which presents were for each of us since none of them had names marked on them.

I did not recognize most of the guests. My mother was there, but not my father. Both of her parents were there. I had never met his parents and didn't ask him to point them out to me; I don't really know if they attended at all. All of the guests were still breathing, I checked. I was unsure at first because of this whirring feeling in my head. And they were sleeping very stiff. They were all wearing party hats with little designs of cakes, candles, and candy on them, and they said *happy birthday* in bubbled fonts, over and over again.

She had to stand on a wooden chair to reach the ceiling and move it carefully around the room, so as not to knock any of our sleeping party-goers and leave bruises on them or, worse, wake them up. I stood awkwardly next to the presents, watching her do this, covering my right eye with my right hand.

He touched the back of my neck with wet egg yolk still on his hands and said: Happy birthday. I turned around and asked him: How old are we now?

He stared at me blankly for a moment before vomiting on my t-shirt, holding his stomach and continuing his sickness onto the living room carpet, onto the guests, spewing out lightbulbs, all of which were lit. My mother woke up when vomit hit her, looking around at all these glowing lightbulbs covered in stomach fluid laying on the floor, all of the dead party guests, the mess of the house, up Sarah's dress, into the attic, into the back of my eyelids, screaming frantically until she finally stopped, immediately, and went back to sleep so suddenly that I thought her heart had stopped beating.

Smoke started to rise out of the kitchen from the oven, the cake burning, and he kept throwing up, Sarah standing there not looking at either of us, all of her attention devoted to hanging the stars, and me standing there having no idea what to do with anything, not even knowing how old I was, how old any of us were, or how we got to this terrible party in the first place.

He had a ring of milk around his mouth. The ladder leading to the attic looked longer than the length of me and shorter than the river. I stared at him from the bottom of it, looking up into the wooden room above me filled with heat and milk. I will turn the lights off, he offered, extending his hand to help me up. I told him to leave the lights on.

I ascended the ladder which was also ascending the breaking of my body somehow. When I reached the top, he handed me a glass of milk. Decisions were not made between us. We did not ever discuss what we were doing, or planned on doing. We drank the milk and glue and did not need to open our mouths again. Our top teeth grew into our bottom teeth and formed a mouth shield.

Sometimes we would argue, grunting, about which one of us had more hair on his body. The arguments about this grew less frequent over time as it became more obvious visually. As it became easier to smell the hair growing under the arms, thicker on the legs, briefly over and around the mouth.

The shield protected us from needing to say what we really wanted to. So we did this: exchanged the body instead of words. And then we would watch the window. From the attic, we saw her helping her father re-paint the garage door on her house and eating popsicles in the yard.

Once she asked me if we could leave the lights on, but I unplugged the lamp from the wall entirely, taking her instead in the black, rubbing the shield of my mouth against her chest, and her the entire time shouting out the dictionary like she memorized it to fill in the silence.

I had a vision of her giving birth to the horse. I was standing in the stables and she was shaking, violently, as if to remove her skin in slices. Her water broke into the hay, glistening, then. And the dead horse came out of her. He was holding her arms and telling her to breathe. She was screaming: My mother's dress is ruined. Between two horses.

I dug my hands underneath my t-shirt and felt at the three long scars going vertical on the right side of my stomach. The horse, dehydrated and shriveled, moved its hind legs in the dirt like it was trying to get up, limply. He pulled her arms back so she couldn't touch it; she shook harder, trying to escape him, trying to hold the horse. It looked up at him and then back towards me, and said: It was him.

I held the horse's head against the knives on my stomach. There, it tried to suck blood out of me as if milk, but the wounds had already healed over, and nothing came out of me. He put his tongue in her ear and she started singing very quietly: *The room just filled up with mosquitoes they heard that my body was free.*

What was left of the treehouse was also burned with the Power Company Building, because that's where we left it, except a few of the lamps, which I had kept in the attic, and which were infected now. Daisies tried to grow out of them from where the wires ended. I asked them both if they had kept any of the lamps for themselves, and they both in unison lifted their clothes to show me three tally mark scars on the right sides of their stomachs.

We put the horse back in her for the night. We all moved in and out of stables, stability, horses. She was bursting with more of them for days, we couldn't stop them, couldn't kill them fast enough. All of them drained of water, all of them dead. Yearning for milk we did not have. And they came out of her, of him, me, each other, full of bullets, full of bleach, covering the floors of the barn, trying to walk out into the wilderness alone looking for mothers impossibly in the arced shapes of trees, crop circles, lakes, ash.

Unresolved: I woke up with certain amounts of fluid in my mouth that came from nowhere, that came from something during sleep. As in: I was pulling something directly from another source into me, which I then swallowed and heaved the next morning. As in: where did it come from, how am I sharing it, how is it being transferred to me. I knew that I had metal in me because there were constant alarms and warnings of this. My mouth was always filled with silver saliva, my whole head caving. The metal in my stomach stung like I had swallowed all of the bees I could find and let them have the honey and peanut butter sandwiches sitting inside me, too. I asked them if they would remove the metal, but this was impossible for them to grasp. I woke up in remote parts of town with no shoes on, my feet covered in my own blood from bad road work, from walking hours lingering unconscious. I said to the doctor, I told her: I looked into North like he told me to and that's what's doing it, but why these gifts, why now. She said: Has anyone noticed you doing this, you know, this walking off while you're sleeping. I said: No one else has said so except North, which is trying to get me to follow it. Is north a codename for one of your friends, she asked, and I shot her a glance so hard I almost knocked myself over.

A holy moment happened between us in one of the public restrooms at the park. He had just come back from the woods, sticks still in his hair, scrapes on his legs, and said he had them in him, as many as possible for all hours of the night, but he couldn't feel it anymore. He could no longer be hunted was how he put it. He said: The only thing I can feel anymore is the energy, and you, and Sarah. He admitted to me what had happened between them. He whispered: We were almost one, if we hadn't kept so many secrets, it would have been possible. I asked him about the fire. I wanted to know why he had done it. And, leaning against the wall enclosure of the bathroom stall, he told me: I thought maybe I could cure us all, I really thought I could do it, you have to believe me.

The three of us stood in the middle of the generators. We spoke volumes without words. We told each other all of our secrets with the only language that we knew: the energy, the sickness, the sleeplessness, the slipping away of identities, our individual selves. I asked her about blind spots, if she had them. Could she see everything or were there parts, just small spaces of things, missing, lost in between transitions from one organism to another. I could see the dresses she had discarded all over the floor, yes. And her belly, full of blizzards, scorching against my legs and inner thighs, and the piercing sound of an entire flock of birds trying to enter me through the ears. Her mother's dresses were levitating above the other ones somehow. The pockets of his pants were overflowing with extra lightbulbs. Yes, I see everything, she said, looking at the two of us, trying to figure out whose pair of what was whose, all of our clothes tangled on the same floor, of the same house, with the lights off and no one wishing they would be on, our eyes adjusting to the darkness, barely, all things around us coming apart. Parts of his t-shirts becoming her legs, my jeans his skull, her dresses my forearms. And sometimes I was him and she was me, and the three of us were in the bedroom, which was flooded, and the three of us were in the attic, which was burned, and the three of us were filling up the houses with lights left on while everyone fell asleep watching television.

She took me night fishing on her father's boat without his permission. It was dangerous because the boat didn't have any lights on it. From where we were out on the lake, we could see just tiny dots of light in the distance, and the moon and stars above. Like someone cut holes in my head to see them. Fortunately, she didn't know any constellations or where the North Star was, so she couldn't point them out to me. Instead, we invented our own. One of them was the Power Company Building. Another was the river. Another was the three of us as fish, scattered among other space debris. She tied our feet to the boat and said: If there's a storm we'll both go down together.

We threw the fish that we caught back. It was easier at night because we didn't have to see their faces. There was just the sensation of their wet skin on our hands, flipping around everywhere in the boat, splashing water.

Hundreds of living organisms were beneath us, all living in the darkness, all blind most of the time, feeling out their food with smell. The two of us were blind fish also. The three of us were caught fish released back into the ocean. He was fucking whales in the woods.

I was seasick once we got back to the shore. I blacked out. I woke up and they were both on one of the mattresses next to me, her with most of what he carried between his legs in her mouth, him biting down hard on a stick to keep quiet. I kept quiet, too. I located my own body attached to me and looked back up at the stars, interrupted by the branches of trees. One of them was the North Star. One of them was all of the fish we threw back into the lake. All of the stars were looking for me as if I could be found.

Each of us was a constellation of dead fish. Each of us was stuck in the sky, which was really just water. He was all of the suns that made the plants which fed us grow. I collected my belongings from inside of her stomach. She had stolen them, over the years, without my knowing. Some of these belongings were the words I'd been trying to say. Others were the ones I was able to conjure. The rest of my language was somewhere between the Power Company Building and North.

She was sharks tattooing the two of us slowly. I absently joined the two of them on the mattress, knowing very well that nothing more could be made from our meat. All of our fluid had been spoiled, anyway.

I went to the Power Company Building again after they had started to rebuild it. Even though it had been a while since the fire. The trees had barely grown back. I lay between the two main generators, except now it didn't seem to do anything. I adjusted several times, trying variations of the position and location I used to know well, but the stomach ache wouldn't go away.

My stomach was full of hard metal and fire. I held the lightbulb gift between my teeth and waited, but it didn't charge up. I thought maybe that the lightbulb had just been burnt out, so I went home and hid in the attic with one of the lamps from the old treehouse. I put the lightbulb into the socket. It lit up. I covered all of the windows in the attic so that no one would know what I was doing. I waited for the light to burn out but gave up after thirty-seven hours when my mother called me for dinner.

Sarah knew well enough to know what I had been doing. She asked me if I had been eating lightbulbs. I accused her of eating the horses. He held the ladder that both of us were on, and we handed the lamp from one to the other, back up and down from the house to the attic.

I wasn't hungry for anything. The doctor asked me if I was sleeping better with the pills she'd been giving me. I said I couldn't remember.

All three of us built a house that we lived in. All three of us at the same time. It was made mostly out of the things that both him and her had saved, documented, of us. When my voice came out of me, it was hers and his was mine. Hers was his. This exchange happened for a while. None of what came out of us was words, just voices. Just singing. No songs.

There were no lamps in our new house. We wanted to keep the lights off. In the dark, it was easier not to know anything. To have to look one another in the eye would have been impossible.

We found him there again, near the broken bricks, with his head wide open. His skull was full of insects and breadcrumbs. Sarah was oscillating between charred rocks where we had left pieces of our knee scrapings, our kites that flew away. I put the lightbulb into his open skull. I waited for it to light up. I waited for the trees to bend down to the ground and scrape away the grass from the lawns. None of this happened. When I realized this, I collapsed. I didn't throw up, even though my stomach felt like I had swallowed rocks. And the insects crawled between her arms and mine, the grass fell lower, all of the electricity scathing across the water. He handed me the blood from his head and said nothing. Down to the lake we went, again.

A subject in a room for a portrait by the nude wall with extra skin around the body, tight. I imagined that Sarah had batteries in her spit, and when I pulled them out, they were warm again like I knew they were inside of her, and I arranged them with the eggs and bacon. Pull them three by three, recharge them. Catching her in the shower singing, I put the batteries between my toes, with the wrong muscles, all of them scattering from me, like insects to the walls.

She masturbates to 1995 electronic dance music. He has gasoline ready for college down. I am changing the bedsheets to make the room colder.

I hold the glass of milk in my bare paws, trying very hard not to spill it, not to get it on the rugs. Calcium this and calcium that, my bones were still breaking, I can't stand up.

I keep the lights off when I enter her and then I cannot tell the difference. Between him and her. The distance between two subjects posing by the nude wall, symmetrical, leaves me. And this is only a violence to myself, and it does not matter. The batteries rolled left on the floor because of the slant and stuck there. Both of the firepits are lit, all of the snow in the kitchen sink is molasses, all of the liquor in the basement is linen. She hides the saxophone in the closet behind the ladder to the attic. I am sitting at the top of the house imagining what the bottom would look like if I reversed it. He is panting ice cream drool onto my knuckles as I rub his bones clean of any harm. I tell him: I am sick, can you see it, and the doctor doesn't know what I should do.

He gives me an Oxford Dictionary and tells me to look up the word: North. The definition said that the three of us were sleeping in the same room even though we had our own, that we all shared the same refrigerator, we were all out of milk. I looked for it between rooms.

She says: If I am positive of what is in my lungs, can I give it to you. I say: I want it anyway, you don't have to ask. He holds her head up from the garden and says: These weeds, why do you keep the weeds. We swim in the pool even though it is drained.

We change the lightbulbs at night to get rid of gathering moths, leaving dust on the light, clouding it. The basement is filled with telephone wires, and all of the milk is stale in our mouths. Two subjects in a room are trying to be solid. When I look in the bedroom, they are putting their bodies back together, and I am putting my own into books. They ask me if I can go out for more milk, and I say: Dad will do it.

A subject in a room is me pushing myself against the wall and waiting for the wall to allow me to be inside of it, to accept that I have never been one solid. They put their bodies back together, and I put my body back into the books. I recite them aloud while they enter me, then, in response.

Three subjects in one room are too many to fit into one room. And three is not symmetry? Three subjects in three rooms doing all separate acts from one another's subjectivity. The violence between him and her and I. The volumes between him and her and I as identities, shouting all through the house. From the top of it, I look down and see her saxophone, her singing.

He is carrying all our clothes down into the laundry room to clean them. There are welts and open places in his head, walking. She is filling his head with the liquor, the linen. And trying to get inside of the refrigerator to make his skin colder, to freeze it into ice, but he leaves and turns the stove on, putting his empty head onto the burner.

I pull the mask off my face in the backyard and bang my head against the bottom of the pool until the milk comes back out of my stomach, all white and thick chunks of it coming out of me. I imagine that it was once warm inside of me and arrange it with the eggs and bacon, throw out the old cartons, fill up the house with sand.

ACKNOWLEDGEMENTS

My unending gratitude to:

Kristina and Jonathan and Sticks and Mitch and Tara and Adam and Meghan and Sara and Jaci and Sandra and Dunja, for careful reading and thoughtful advice during edits of this book in its many fragmented stages, for being encouraging even when it felt like this thing would never come together, for advice on all of the big questions that loom in this text.

Tarsila, for her big heart, for afternoons sewing and embroidering the cover of this book.

Jason, for continually being brave with and for me in these volatile years, for explaining structural differential and helping me attempt to grasp the rational world, and for simultaneously understanding that the body will always remain a mystery to me.

Mike, most of all, for his willingness to get into my skull and dig around, for believing in this text and its many questions, for trying to provide answers, for support and friendship every step of the way.

JORDAAN MASON is a filmmaker, musician, and writer. They live in Toronto with their husband and their cats.

Made in United States
North Haven, CT
26 September 2022

24575108R00146